FEBRUARY'S ROAD

Also by John Verney
Friday's Tunnel

FEBRUARY'S ROAD

JOHN VERNEY

Illustrated by the author

Collins

William Collins Sons & Co Ltd
London · Glasgow · Sydney · Auckland
Toronto · Johannesburg

First published 1961
© John Verney 1961
First published in this edition 1987

Verney, John
February's road.
I. Title
823'.914[J]   PZ7

ISBN 0–00–184251–X

Printed and bound in Great Britain
by Robert Hartnoll (1985) Ltd, Bodmin

For Sabrina

AUTHOR'S NOTE

In *February's Road* most of the characters who were introduced in *Friday's Tunnel* reappear, but both they and the situations are entirely fictitious and have no possible connection with real life

Chapter 1

THE FIRST SIGN of impending disaster, the first puff of wind, so to speak, in the storm about to turn our quiet valley into the centre of a National Scandal, came on the Fifth Day of Christmas which was a Wednesday.

My father's own holiday ended that morning and he gobbled an early breakfast before catching the fast train from Querbury, when Friday (who is my elder brother) brought in the mail— a great pile of it held up by the Christmas chaos. There were a few letters for us all but the bulk was Daddy's. He adores letters, anything in a properly stuck down envelope so long as it's not a bill or a Christmas card, which he hates. These were all bills or Christmas cards and we watched the gloom descend as he glanced at them disgustedly.

His name is Augustus Callendar and a newspaper Profile once described him as " a strongly emotional personality who always keeps his powerful feelings under control." By the Fifth Day of Christmas the control has worn pretty thin.

We'd had a super Christmas as always—our mother sees to that, and Daddy had done his best to enter into the seasonal spirit. But the truth is he hates the whole thing because it dislocates his work for weeks before and after. This year it had put him behind schedule with a series of articles for the *Messenger* on the need to build really good modern roads and he had been expecting a letter for days with photos and statistics about a new trunk road in Lancashire or somewhere. Now, when he found the letter *still* hadn't arrived, he swore loudly and chucked all the envelopes and their contents in the air. The bits of paper fluttered down like giant snowflakes on to the remains of breakfast, upsetting a milk jug.

My mother is calm in all circumstances—probably her feelings aren't so powerful. Without glancing up from her mail she said quietly, " Someone fetch a rag before it goes through the tablecloth. Here's a card from Hal Fawcett, and it's too awful because I believe we forgot to send one to him."

Gail, the next to me in age and the helpful member of the family, nipped off to fetch the rag. The rest of us just sat silent and embarrassed because we realised that Daddy hadn't done it as a joke, but was really and truly and absolutely and utterly FED UP.

We realised it even more when he said venomously, as if every word was a deadly blow aimed to kill some loathsome reptile : " If all the time and money and energy and thought and bad temper wasted on the sordid commercialisation of the world's most sacred festival could be harnessed, they would carry a rocket to the moon. And I for one would gladly travel on it, so long as I could be *certain* they don't have Christmas there too." That made him feel better because he smiled more like himself, and said : " My apologies," and began to collect the envelopes, wiping butter and porridge from some of them.

Then we all relaxed and teased him about being so bald, until Mummy said : " The post *is* haywire this year. Here's a week-old letter from those people called Gumble who've just moved into Fitchetts."

"Fitchetts," I said. "That's the big ugly house on the Chichester road where the meet is to-morrow."

"Gumble . . ." Daddy licked marmalade from the corner of the electricity bill. "Wasn't there a gallery off Bond Street?"

"Yes, I exhibited a few pictures there just after the war. This one is Captain Gumble—Army not Navy. No relation, I imagine. I ran into Mrs. Gumble shopping in Querbury about a month ago. We got talking and I introduced myself. Perhaps I never told you. Surely you know whom I mean?"

"Not a clue, actually."

"Of course, you never read the local paper. He's on the Council and the only one who ever *does* anything. I believe he owns a lot of property in and around Querbury, and has a finger in all the local pies; a real go-getter from what I've heard, and aims to become our M.P. when old Crump fades out which can't be long. Probably not quite your type, but I'd love to meet him to ask what the Council intends to do about that ghastly corner in Brampton. They've invited us for a drink on the 29th. That's to-day, isn't it?"

My father looked as if he might lose control again. "Oh, NO. I get little enough time at home and what I do get is largely spent driving the children to and from parties, without having to rush out unnecessarily on a cold wet night to meet someone I detest."

Mummy doesn't drive a car, and he certainly had chauffeured for us a lot in the past ten days.

Friday looked innocently at the ceiling. "How can you detest him if you've only just heard of him?"

"Yes, how?" we all cried, seeing he was now in a mood to be laughed at.

" Something tells me I will detest him. I know the type. *Captain* Gumble. Spent a couple of years in the war as some sort of bogus contractor to the R.A.S.C. and has clung to the rank ever since. So useful in business. Ditto local politics."

" That was rather unworthy of you," Mummy said icily. " And I think you should be more careful what you say in front of the children about someone you haven't even met."

" Oh, all right. I expect he's a splendid chap. Anyway, what was the wife like? "

" Roughly my age. Quite pretty in a dim way. She was wearing a genuine mink coat and Paris hat. A bit incongruous, buying kippers in Macfish, which is why I thought she looked amusing and spoke to her. They lived in Querbury for ten years and bought Fitchetts six months ago. She said they hoped to be in by Christmas and would get in touch. Well, they are and they have, if you follow me. I think it would be unfriendly not to go, especially as we haven't answered."

" How could we have answered? Besides, we can't abandon a houseful of children."

" I'll ask Mrs. Mitchell to sit in. I know she'd welcome a chance to leave her home for an hour or two. And so would I . . ." she added meaningly, as Daddy was about to raise a further objection.

He sighed. " Oh, well, I'll make some excuse at the office and catch the earlier train. I should be back here by six-fifteen. What time do they want us? "

" Six-thirty onwards. It's only fifteen minutes' drive. You can pick us up and go straight on. We'll be waiting and ready."

" We? "

" Yes, Mrs. Gumble has kindly asked Friday and Feb too.

She says several people will be bringing children of their age and she has a nephew staying for the holidays who is at Boreham." Mummy looked at the letter again. "His name is Peter Blow, I think. Or does she mean that in the sense of Blast? Her writing is terrible."

"Blow . . ." Daddy said. "I wonder if he's the son of Jasper Blow, the new Minister of Highways."

Of course I had begun to protest at once. I always do protest about meeting fresh people, though I admit I usually enjoy myself once there. But Friday, who is much more sociable, seemed now to be horror struck at the idea.

"Not P. Blow!" he said, as if he had a violent stomach pain. "Not *Blow*! Oh, no, I absolutely refuse to come and meet Blow."

"But why ever not? Do you know him at Boreham then?" asked Mummy.

"Not exactly *know* him. He's Head of my House."

Friday had only been at Boreham two terms and it amazed us how shy he had become about meeting other boys from the school if they happened to be a year or two older. (Before that he was at the same co-ed school as me in Yorkshire, where none of us worry two hoots about anyone, whatever their age!)

"But surely that's splendid, if he's in your House," Mummy insisted. "Perhaps he asked his aunt specially to ask you."

"*Very* likely, I don't think," Friday growled, and went on muttering rebelliously.

Daddy laughed. "I can appreciate the niceties of the dilemma rather more than you, my dear. All the same, Friday, you'd better come along as you're invited. You may have a chance to drop a cocktail down his neck or something. Well, I must fly."

He kissed Mummy and, as he left the room, turned to Friday again. " I'd hate you to overtire yourself unduly, young man, but your task for to-day *might* be to remove those revolting balloons from the ceiling."

" That certainly would overtire me," Friday said.

Chapter 2

WE LIVE in a converted farmhouse called Marsh Manor, two miles from the nearest village Brampton, six from Querbury and about ten from Chichester. The River Quer meanders past down our valley and eventually flows into Chichester Harbour. Marsh Manor is reached by a winding lane and nestles under the side of Querbury Beacon, one of the most famous beauty spots on the South Downs and, unlike most of the others, only reachable on foot or horseback.

Apart from Friday and me, there's Gail who is nearly twelve, then Berry, Chrys and Des spaced out roughly two years apart. Their full names are generally considered so awful I won't reveal them. And there's a baby brother, rather more than a year old at that time, called Hildebrand. You can assume he was named after the Pope or after the horse, depending on the sort of person you are. I prefer to think it was after the horse—because that's the sort of person I am.

We have eight acres of garden and paddock, which my father calls a Small Holding for Income Tax purposes, because then he can claim the car, the gardener's wages and a few other things as Legitimate Expenses. Occasionally we sell surplus eggs and vegetables. We also keep a house cow called Jane, but we don't sell milk because that needs a special licence and involves you in various complications. But for a month or two after calving Jane gives four gallons—far more than we need. So we set it all for cream and butter, and give away the skimmed milk to our nearest neighbours, half a dozen oldish people in cottages down the lane. Usually they buy their milk from Mr. Bunn, our local farmer, and we suspect he or his wife made a fuss—we never learnt for sure. But soon after we had given away the skimmed milk the first time, an inspector of something called and said we had no business to supply milk without a licence. Daddy explained that if we didn't do that we would have to pour it down the drain.

"In that case," the inspector said, "you should not draw off more milk at a time than you can consume."

Daddy passed the story on to Mike Spillergun for his column in the *Messenger* and the inspector never came again, though we continued giving the milk away for the short overflow period each year. This Christmas Jane was dry, and that was a relief because nothing casts such a blight on the Christmas hols as having to bring her in twice daily through slush, snow or whatever.

Personally, I agree with my father that the best part of Christmas comes in advance. The *looking forward* to it when you're at school; the wrapping and sending of presents, the decoration of the tree, the hanging up of chains and garlands and stockings, etcetera, when you're at home. In short, that delicious feeling of anticipation which reaches its climax last thing on Christmas Eve when you go to bed expecting something terrific to happen, something *more* than stockings and turkeys and so forth, super fun though those are.

Well, to be honest, nothing *does* happen, does it? Nothing, I mean, which you hadn't known would happen, once you're old enough to remember what other Christmases were like.

And then there are all those thank-you letters for presents
which lost their charm ten minutes after you opened them.
Even the ones you'd especially asked for seem like a big mistake
on someone's part, probably yours. And then again there's the
tidying up—a time when you're always tripping over bits of
disused string or finding tartan sticky tape in the soup; a time,
at least in our home, when the Hoover drones almost cease-
lessly day and night, sucking up holly berries, nuts, tinsel, glass
splinters and nameless sticky messes from the carpet. We're
taught at school that nature abhors a vacuum. Well, my nature
abhors a vacuum cleaner.

This Christmas was no exception. By the Wednesday we
were all as deflated as the clusters of balloons which my father
had lost his temper fixing to the dining-room ceiling a week
before. They hung there now like bunches of shrivelled
peppers, only no one could be fagged to fetch the step-ladder
to remove them. And at least one reason for our depression
was the thought, lurking at the back of all our minds, that the
ghastly ordeal of our DANCE lay a fortnight ahead.

The dance was my mother's idea. She wrote to Friday and
me at school, saying we had already been asked to several
parties in the coming hols, that you can't go on accepting
other people's hospitality without returning it and that our
mess-room in the barn would be ideal if properly cleaned out.
At the distance of school I hadn't minded so much. I had even
sent along a few names of girls I could face seeing again at
home, if they could face finding their way to our remote
corner of the Sussex Downs. Friday had done likewise. And
now there the dance was, a *fait accompli* as the Dutch say, the
invitations long since sent, a caterer booked, a new gramophone
and records hired—and the mess-room of course still to be

cleaned out. We hated the whole idea; and were secretly rather pleased about it too, as you can be. And once Christmas was over we groaned and grumbled at Mummy about it continually, though generally she was too busy Hoovering to hear what we said. Besides, she's well used to groans and grumbles and doesn't appear to mind.

"Don't be so silly. It will be lovely fun. You wait," was her invariable answer.

Whereas Daddy, depending on his mood, either told us to shut up or else said, " Of *course* it will be a flop, but it will give you something to talk about when you're back at school."

I suppose he understands Friday and me pretty well in most things, but he just does *not* seem to realise that we do *not* like to be reminded about going back to school when we're at home.

After he'd left for London that Wednesday morning we all mooched around, waiting for Mummy to finish clearing the breakfast before we started on the groaning and grumbling. I wondered what Friday would do about the balloons because I knew, and he knew, that actually our father would be jolly cross if he came back and found he had in fact done nothing about them. In years gone by my brother was the most energetic person I've ever met, always digging tunnels or something. But this hols he seemed to have lost all his energy and spent every day lying on his bed and just growing.

That Wednesday, however, he exerted himself and passed the whole morning seeing if he was tall enough to jump and reach the withered balloons from the dining-room floor. I tried to catch up on thank-you letters in the living-room next door and could hear the sound of him jumping even above the sound of the Hoover. The whole house shook and once a

picture crashed, but that was on the landing above, where
Gail, Berry, Chrys and Des were being the Covent Garden
Ballet. Hildebrand, asleep in his cot, woke up and yelled.
Altogether I didn't write many letters.

About lunch-time I abandoned what my father calls "a
salutary exercise in insincerity," and went to see how Friday
had got on. There were only two balloons left dangling from
the staple. He was stretched out on the floor, gathering
strength, he said, for a supreme effort while he giggled over
Mike Spillergun's column in yesterday's *Messenger*.

The column, which comes out Tuesdays and Thursdays, is
packed with crazy jokes but underneath there's always a serious
purpose, spotlighting some abuse or exposing a racket, with
the deadliest of all weapons—ridicule. My father says there's
nothing else quite like it in English journalism. The nearest
equivalent would be one of the American columnists—which
is not surprising, for Mike Spillergun was born in the States
and became a British subject in the war. (I believe his father
was called Schpiffelerghun or something of that kind and
migrated to the U.S.A. from Finland or Denmark or somewhere of that sort.)

He's especially funny about politicians—unless you happen
to be the one concerned—and he's been sued once or twice
for libel, but without success, because he always takes infinite
trouble to be accurate on matters of *fact*. Personally, at the
time I'm describing, I found his column rather dull but
Friday, since going to Boreham, had developed a tiresome
appreciation for grown-up, or as he called it *adult*, humour
and in this respect Mike Spillergun was his hero of the moment.

" Tee-hee," he giggled. " Oh, I say, that's delightful."

" What is? " I asked, doubting whether I would agree.

"He's taken a crack at our M.P. He says the Member for Querbury should be called 'Notwithstanding' Crump from his habit of sitting on any available fence."

I still couldn't see that it was so funny, when my mother came in to lay the table. Friday showed her his morning's work with pride.

"Darling, you are a great help," she said, putting a dish of cold sliced turkey and the remains of the stuffing on the centre of the tablecloth. " But wouldn't it be easier if you stood on the table?"

" I thought you didn't like me standing on the table. You always say it scratches the top."

" Well, you could put a newspaper or cushion. Why not fetch the step-ladder? It's out in the barn, I remember. Daddy started on the decorations for the dance last night."

" Not worth it. I can easily reach the last two. The string snaps off and the staple may as well stay there for next year."

Friday crouched and gave a mighty leap, his right hand closing round both balloons. For a second he was actually hanging. Then he came down with the string and staple as well. And the next second five square feet of plaster crashed on to the table. The stuffing was too mixed with plaster to be eatable but we salvaged some of the turkey.

Chapter 3

AFTER LUNCH Gail and I decided to visit Jane and the ponies in the paddock, before walking up on to the downs. I loathe walking, but it's better than writing thank-you letters or looking after the little ones, which were the alternatives. Normally we would have gone for a ride, but we needed to rest our ponies before the hunt.

Friday wanted to help Mr. Mitchell, who lives with his wife in Brampton and comes to us daily as our gardener. He's a brilliant handyman and thought he could patch the ceiling, at least well enough for my father not to notice. Daddy is hopelessly unobservant about interior decoration, in fact he wouldn't notice if the whole house was repainted in his absence. What he does know *instantly* is if a book has changed place on the shelves, because it's always the one book he wants in a hurry.

Gail and I left Friday and Mr. Mitchell stirring their mixture in the dining-room, watched by the younger girls who were supposed to help Mummy stir batter for drop scones in the kitchen. They were also supposed to keep an eye on Hildebrand, the demon crawler. We fetched oats to give Gorse and the Grey Arab. (I had had the latter eighteen months, but we'd never been able to agree on a suitable name, so he was still called the Grey Arab.) We found the two larger ponies sheltering in the shed, while Jane and Clover, our old Shetland pony, grazed side by side in the paddock. We shook up fresh bedding, warned them they would be expected to do a hard day's work to-morrow and set off on the track towards the quarry.

Half the time Gail's so buttoned up and sort of efficient you can't tell what she's thinking because she doesn't speak, just gets on with things. But sometimes she likes to chatter more than any of us, particularly when she and I are alone, and this was one of those times.

" Have you decided what you're going to be when you grow up? " she asked, as we plodded through the chalky mud of the lane.

" Of course. I've told you a million times. I shall be a riding instructor and have a school of my own and breed show ponies."

" But how will you get the money? "

"Dunno. I shall find it somehow. Anyway, you don't need much to start with. I expect Daddy will lend me what I need."

"I don't think Daddy has much to spare, really. I heard him discussing it with Mummy the other day. I mean, it must cost an awful lot having so many children, especially sending you and Friday to private schools."

" Why does he send us then? I don't learn anything which is going to be useful as a riding instructor, except perhaps a few sums. 'If eight horses eat a hundredweight of oats a month, how many oats will twenty horses eat in a year?' That sort of thing."

" You might need French, if you have French people at your school."

" I don't intend to have French people at my school."

" Some French people are jolly good riders."

" Well, if they want to come to my school they'll have to be jolly good at English too."

" Wasn't it funny at breakfast when Daddy got so cross with all those bills and threw them into the air? He was really cross, wasn't he?"

" Yup. He was. I expect it was just Christmas blues like he always gets, or else he's worried about something. He's always worried about something. Mummy says that's how he's made."

" I wonder if I'll have worries when I grow up."

" Depends what you're going to be. Have you decided yet?"

When you ask her a personal question Gail has a funny way of blushing and screwing her face with a little giggle which is rather sweet, only it annoys me.

" I think I shall just be a Mummy," she said, after much thought.

" Golly, what a soppy ambition," I said. And of course that hurt her feelings so we didn't speak again till we reached the quarry.

In the December afternoon gloom there was an eerie feeling about the deserted quarry. The semicircle of chalk cliff hung like a shroud faintly reflected in the pond below, which always fills up in winter. It was the sort of place you instinctively lower your voice. And the effect of spookiness was increased by great festoons of old man's beard covering the bushes at the entrance.

" Where does the stuff *come* from, whatever it's called," I asked. " You never notice it the rest of the year."

"Oh yes you do if you look properly. We picked some on a nature walk at school last summer. It's wild clematis or traveller's joy."

Gail and the other girls go to the village school in Brampton. It costs nothing, a special bus is even sent to collect them every morning, and they are always learning interesting new facts, especially about Nature. Whereas the schools Friday and I go to cost a packet, including expensive train fares, and we never seem to learn anything. It's all very puzzling, as the monkey said stuck half-way up the *araucaria imbricata*.

Occasionally a gipsy family camp at the quarry but there was no sign of them now.

"Why isn't the quarry used any more?" Gail said. "We could have such fun watching them work it and there must be masses of chalk still left."

"I know. I've often thought the same. I've heard Daddy say the war stopped the quarrying and afterwards the company went broke and sold out."

"Mr. Bunn doesn't own it now, does he?"

"No, his land ends at Marsh Manor, I believe. Actually, I've often wondered who *does* own all this land."

"I never understand about *owning* land, do you? I mean, we can't ride across fields without asking permission but no one seems to mind us riding over the downs. I imagined they sort of belonged to the public."

"No, I think they belong to someone, like everything else. Lord Sprockett has the woods on the far side of Querbury Beacon, but I'm pretty sure he doesn't own any of the land on this side. Of course you see Mr. Bunn's sheep and cattle up here sometimes, but I think he rents the grazing."

"That's another thing I don't understand. About renting. For instance, does Daddy own Marsh Manor or does he rent it from someone else?"

"No, he bought it outright. At least, I think he did."

"It must have cost an awful lot. How much? About two hundred pounds?"

"Two hundred! More like two thousand, you ass."

"Two thousand! I shouldn't have thought he had all that."

"Well, you don't have to pay for your house in one go. You can pay gradually, like hire-purchasing a TV set. And then it becomes yours eventually."

"But what happens if you suddenly *can't* pay any more—I mean, after you have already paid about half?"

"No idea. You lose the TV set I do know, so I suppose you lose the house too. Anyway, I'm sure Daddy *has* paid for Marsh Manor by now, even if he didn't buy it with a lump sum to start with."

"I *suppose* so," Gail said rather doubtfully.

We wandered on, and threw a few stones in the pond.

Probably there was always a spring at this point on the downs, but two hundred years ago the hillside was dug out as a reservoir to supply the Dippen-Quer canal with water. The canal craze had just started, and one was built to join the river Quer with the river Dippen which flows to the north of Querbury Beacon. A two-mile tunnel was driven through the downs and a drain from the reservoir fed water into it. One end of the tunnel started in Dippenhall, on the land owned at present by Lord Sprockett, of Sprocketts, Ltd. (and a good deal else); the other end came out at Marsh Manor.

But the whole canal was abandoned early in the nineteenth century, the tunnel entrances collapsed and were overgrown and the reservoir became the chalk quarry. The canal's existence had been virtually forgotten for a hundred years when Friday, in his energetic digging phase, accidently unearthed our end of it eighteen months ago.

There was a great hoo-ha about its rediscovery, and to my brother's utter disgust, the entrance was sealed up again for safety. Since then there has been a lively public campaign to put the canal back into working order. The leading spirit is a friend of ours, an engineering student called Robin Fawcett. He maintains, and a lot of people have written to the papers supporting him, that even if the Dippen-Quer canal couldn't hope to *make* money, at least it wouldn't *lose* more than British Railways and that, like B.R., it would still be well worth preserving as a national amenity. Even our M.P., Sir Gilbert Crump, came off his fence for once and raised the idea in Parliament. On the other hand, the Querbury Urban District Council, for their own mysterious reasons, were dead against it. The last I had heard was that Robin had persuaded Lord Sprockett to pay half the cost if the Government would pay the other half.

I had meant all the hols to ask for the latest news, but Christmas put it out of my head. Being in the quarry put it back.

" Anything more happened about Robin's canal? "

" Don't think so. He stayed one week-end before you and Friday came home. I think Lord Sprockett has rather lost interest. So has the Government, because it needs all its money for making bombs and roads and more important things like that."

" Huh."

" I'm afraid Robin has rather lost interest too. He finishes his degree this summer and then he wants to build a dam in India. Besides, there isn't really much *point* in opening up the canal again, is there? "

" There most certainly is. For one thing, it would be super fun—boating and all that. And, anyway, better canals would help take traffic off the roads."

" Well, there's not an awful lot of traffic to be taken off the roads round here."

"Isn't there just! About fifty people are killed every year between Querbury and Chichester alone and that's nothing to what it will be like in——"

"Oh, look, there's a car," Gail interrupted. "I've never seen one here before."

The car was a Landrover, parked behind a large bramble bush. The letters Q.U.D.C. were painted on its side. "That's odd," she said. "It can only have come here by passing Marsh Manor. I never heard it, did you?"

"Probably too much of a row going on. Anyway, it could have come by the track from Dippenhall over the Saddle. The gipsies' horse pulls their caravan that way sometimes, so a Landrover could easily make it. Or, I suppose, it might have come past Querbury Beacon on the track from Brampton. That's a much more gradual climb though I've never seen a car do it."

"What does Q.U.D.C. stand for?"

"The Urban District Council, of course. You know, they clear the refuse and empty the drains and mend the roads and all that. Daddy has to pay them taxes, only it's called rates."

"I see," Gail said humbly. She's always impressed by my superior knowledge of how the world is organised and it's a pleasure to be able to tell *her* things occasionally.

"What are they doing here?" she added. "There's no road to mend, and no refuse apart from hikers in summer, and no drains except that one to the tunnel Robin found, which is blocked up again now."

"Perhaps they're checking it's still properly blocked up."

But they obviously weren't or we should have seen them and there was no sign of anyone.

" Wouldn't it be super if it was a *stolen* car! We might ask Mummy to ring the police when we get home."

" Oh, ha, ha! " I said. " Probably a dead body in the back too."

All the same, I peeped into the back with just the teeniest tingle of excitement. And had rather more than a teeny fright when a savage-looking boxer, the size of Clover, sat up suddenly and growled. I admit I'm scared of dogs I don't know, but Gail has a way with them. She came up beside me and patted him fearlessly on the head and he sank back, thumping his stub of tail on the truck floor with unexpected friendliness. Otherwise the back was empty save for what looked like a leather box of instruments.

" Let's take him with us for our walk," she said. " Come on, Ginger."

But he just thumped as if to say, " I'd love to, but I've been told to guard this lot and I'm afraid I must." So we left him and followed the track to the top of the quarry. The chalk sides are mostly precipitous but there's one place you can slide more or less safely to the bottom if you have the nerve. On a historic occasion I rode over the edge (by mistake) on the Grey Arab and I always look to see if the marks are still there. They had almost been washed away by now.

" Let's have a go at sliding down." I was a bit nettled by Gail scoring off me over the dog.

" Oh, no, I *daren't*. Besides, we'd make ourselves muddy. It's all wet."

" You're wet," I said, rather glad not to all the same.

After that we discussed whether to climb on towards the

Beacon, but agreed in the end to continue west along the downs, which would give a better view of the country we might hunt over.

Fitchetts is what my mother calls a Victorian horror, a monster of a house in purple brick, bristling with gables and turrets and twisted chimneys. The meet had been there the previous Christmas—our very first hunt. At that time it was lived in by an old colonel who had since died. As we strode along, the house and the surrounding woods lay out of sight beyond hills to the south of the Quer Valley, but I remembered how hounds had run north that day, towards the Quer. I recognised a clump of willows by the river where the hunt had ended and I had sadly turned for home.

A light drizzle had been falling when Gail and I left Marsh Manor, but now the weather cleared. To our front a huge red disc hung just over the farthest edge of the downs and the velvety turf underfoot stretched towards it in one long undulating sweep. It was like walking on the flank of a gigantic green cow peacefully resting in the winter sunlight.

"I'm just so *glad* sometimes we live here now instead of London, aren't you?" said Gail.

"It's not too bad," I muttered, only half attending. I was studying the hedges in the valley below and visualising myself on the Grey Arab sailing over them with the leading hounds, and with the rest of the field strung out *miles* to the rear.

"Let's turn downhill now," I said, " and go home through the fields along the bottom. Then we can look for good places to jump. You can never tell, we may be glad of them tomorrow."

Three men came into view on the hillside a hundred yards away. Two of them, bareheaded and quite young, wore shabby windbreakers and seemed to be measuring something with those red and white poles and an instrument on a tripod. The third was older and much larger. He wore a smart checked cap and overcoat, smoked a pipe and studied what looked like a map pinned to a board. He glanced at us but with no more interest than if we were flies on the ceiling.

" Those must be the men from the Landrover," said Gail. "What are their funny sticks? "

" They use them for making maps, I think. Shall we see what they're doing? "

" No, don't let's. I hate meeting people on walks. You never know whether to talk and it's embarrassing."

"Well, let's just go a little nearer and then turn off downhill, as if that was what we had intended all along."

The two young men began to move their poles but the older one remained looking at the board. He was very tall and large, with an enormous grey bushy moustache, rather like that man whose face is used for advertising beer on the posters. We strode up to within fifty yards, pretending not to be aware of his existence, before casually changing course.

" Splendid afternoon for a walk. Sensible girls," he said suddenly.

I don't suppose he raised his voice, but in the still air it boomed loudly as a cannon. I sort of waved shyly and Gail giggled and we continued downhill feeling a bit foolish.

" Why would they be making a map up there, do you

think?" she asked later, as we scrambled through a hedge near the river.

"Dunno. Probably just keeping things up to date."

"You wouldn't think anything had changed on that down for a hundred years. And I didn't know the District Council

made maps. I remember Robin telling us they are made by the Ord—Ord-something."

"Ordinary Survey," I explained.

It was almost dark and we hurried to reach home before the others ate all the tea. In fact, if we hadn't heard the wonderful swooshing sound, we would have missed seeing the swans. There were seven, two of them whiter than the others. The great flapping shapes, as unreal somehow as huge paper darts,

passed overhead. We heard them land on the Quer with
another swoosh.

"I saw the parents with their five little cygnets this spring,
on one of our school nature walks," Gail said excitedly.
"Goodness, how *large* they've grown."

"Well, you wouldn't expect them to grow *small*, would
you?" I said.

Chapter 4

THE OTHERS had almost finished tea when we arrived, but there was still an uneaten pile of drop scones, soggy in melted butter. Gail doesn't care for them, so I began to wolf the lot. They had a delicious and unusual powdery taste.

" I shouldn't eat *too* many," said my mother. " Some of Mr. Mitchell's plaster got mixed up with the batter by mistake . . ."

" You haven't looked at the ceiling yet," said Friday. Mr. Mitchell had certainly fixed it beautifully. Only a damp patch showed, as if the rain had come through the room above (which it often does) and that would soon dry out. Friday was so pleased with his share of the work that he seemed quite to have forgotten the ordeal of shortly meeting P. Blow. He made out that the ceiling was in fact far stronger now and that the silly accident was therefore entirely to his credit.

" I don't suppose Daddy will look at it that way," I said.

" I'll give you six to four in pennies that Daddy never even notices."

" Make it ten to four in gob stoppers and I'll take you."

" It's a bet."

" I never understand bets," said Mummy. " If Daddy *does* notice who gives whom what?"

"If he doesn't notice then Feb owes me ten gob stoppers. If he *does*, then I owe her four."

"Rubbish. It's the other way round," I cried. "If he *doesn't* notice . . ."

(The argument was never settled. My father *didn't* notice and for the rest of the hols Friday, whenever he wanted to be tiresome, claimed that I owed him ten gob stoppers. Whereas of course he owed *me* ten.)

Tea over, there was a stack of washing-up to be done in the kitchen. So I volunteered to look after Hildebrand while the others did it.

Gail may be better than me with dogs. But I'm better than anyone with Hildebrand, or so I maintain. As soon as we were alone in the dining-room he became a circus pony and I trained him to crawl in and out of the table and chair legs by rewarding him with brown sugar. When he had mastered that I tried him at the sideboard, a huge oak affair with a space about eight inches high underneath. There's a wavy moulding in front almost touching the floor, but the sides are plain and it is *just* possible for a very small child with plenty of guts to crawl through. When it comes to squeezing under things Hildebrand has what it takes and I prophesy that some day he'll win his school obstacle race. He stuck at one point and started to wail, but by alternately prodding him behind with a carving fork and offering him a tablespoonful of brown sugar from in front, I got him out. He had certainly swept that corner of the floor as it hadn't been swept for years and his face, clothes and hair (what he has) were coated with fluff, crumbs and cigarette stubs. There was even a letter wedged in the neck of his overalls.

I guessed it was one of those my father had thrown in the

air at breakfast. It must have glided down under the sideboard
unnoticed. While Hildebrand licked the spoon I glanced
casually at the letter. And then read it very carefully indeed.

It was marked Private and Confidential and was addressed
to my father from Barclay's Bank, Querbury.

" Dear Sir,
    As requested we have paid your cheque for the outstanding
instalments on the mortgage for Marsh Manor to the
mortgagees, the Downland Preservation Company Ltd. This
now brings your overdraft (at the close of to-day's business)
to £1972 10s. 6d., and we understand that you will be
taking steps to remedy this position at your earliest possible
convenience. In this connection we also note that you have
decided to accept an offer by the Downland Preservation
Company to purchase part of your property to enable you
to lift the loan remaining under the mortgage."

The letter was signed with an illegible signature above the word " Manager."

" Golly," I said to Hildebrand. " Your father is nearly two thousand quid in the red. No wonder he seems so worried."

To tell the truth, I was suddenly worried nearly sick myself. What on earth was a mortgage? It sounded like a sentence of death. And what did they mean about the company purchasing part of the property?

But Hildebrand had pulled himself to his feet and was reaching for the bowl of brown sugar on the table.

" No more," I said firmly. " We can't afford it."

He began to yell, so I quickly gave him a piggy back and carried him with me through the living-room to Daddy's study which opens off it. The morning's pile of correspondence lay untidily on his desk. I slipped the bank's letter among the rest. By then the others were filtering back to the hall from the kitchen.

" I'm afraid Hildebrand is in rather a mess," I said, handing him over to Mummy.

" Never mind. I'm just going to bath him. You and Friday had better change and get ready so as not to keep Daddy waiting. Are you all right, darling? You look pale."

" She does, doesn't she? Too many drop scones," said Friday. " All that plaster."

" Of course I was only joking about those," said Mummy. " Sure you feel up to going with us? "

" I'm perfectly O.K.," I said crossly. " I want to go."

And it's just as well for everyone that I went.

Chapter 5

M Y F A T H E R returned punctually at six fifteen as promised, having collected Mrs. Mitchell. Amazingly, I was all dressed and ready. My mother was in the bath and Friday couldn't decide whether to wear a grey flannel suit, the coat of which was two sizes too small, or a new dark blue suit one size too large. Though he wouldn't admit it, he was in a complete flap at the prospect of meeting P. Blow.

" What *does* it matter what you wear? " Mummy kept saying from her bath.

" You look awful either way," I said, having little patience with my brother's clothes complex.

Daddy, carrying a double whisky, came upstairs and joined in the argument.

"I entirely sympathise with you, Friday," he said. "I should wear the trousers off the grey suit with the blue coat. And why not sew brass buttons on it too? You'll look vaguely nautical, at least *sportif*; just the job for Captain Gumble. Lots of time. Your mother won't be ready for hours."

But Friday was in no mood for jokes. Without a word he put on the blue suit, deliberately shrinking himself to make it still larger on him. Then, with an expression of silent but intense martyrdom, he went and sat alone in the car. Twenty minutes later we joined him there and set off for the Gumbles, leaving Mrs. Mitchell in charge.

" It's quite pointless going at all now. The party will be over before we arrive," my father said cheerfully. Usually he hates being kept waiting, but now he was in rather good form —the effect, probably, of having started work again, or perhaps of the whisky.

" How were things at the office?" my mother asked.

" A good day on the whole. I found the letter from York-shire waiting and managed to finish the last article. By the way," he added—and I had the impression that he intended the remark to sound more casual than it was—" Jasper Blow is certainly hotting things up at the Ministry. I lunched with one of his underlings to hear about road policy in general. They've a hush-hush plan to beat all records with a new trunk road to the Portsmouth area."

" Oh? Where's it going?"

" He wouldn't tell me, but vaguely in this direction, I suppose. The Minister, I'm glad to say, has followed the suggestion I made recently in the *Messenger*."

" What sort of suggestion?" I asked.

" Roughly, to treat the road problem as a national emergency —as if there was a war on. Decide on the best possible route and then push ahead full speed and to hell with the usual scream from vested interests."

" If they tried to put the road through some place like Cowdray Park *you* would be the first person to scream . . ." Mummy said sharply. My father thinks Cowdray Park is one of the most perfect stretches of country in England.

" Yes. Because I don't call that the best possible route for a major road. Obviously certain things must be sacred. Still,

roads *are* a vital matter and someone is bound to hate it
wherever you go. In this case I gather the Government intends
to build a ten-mile section at high pressure, to show what it
can do if it wants to. My friend told me they've already
bought the land at a fabulous price by ordinary market rates,
but even so the sum involved is minute compared to what is
spent daily on things like armaments."

We had reached Brampton, where our lane joins the Querbury-Chichester road at a hair-raising bend. There wasn't much traffic at this time of year and you could see the headlights of cars approaching from either direction. But my mother, who once saw a cyclist killed there, always makes a great fuss about stopping and taking a good look. " Do be careful," she exclaimed, drawing in her breath and pressing her feet on to the floor. Nothing annoys my father more. He halted for an exaggerated length of time before cautiously turning south on to the road.

" I do hope you persuade your pal Gumble to straighten that corner, if only to save me going through all this every time I drive you anywhere," he said in exasperation.

Later when our nerves had settled and we whizzed along towards Fitchetts, I asked : " Can the Government just buy up any land it wants ? "

" It amounts to that—at least for work of national importance, like military training areas or airfields or trunk roads. There may have to be a special Act of Parliament, but the Government, and for that matter Local Authorities, already have enormous powers under the various Planning Acts for what's called " compulsory purchase." Of course, they pay the landowners compensation."

" Who decides how much compensation? " Friday asked sourly, speaking for the first time.

" Ah, that's the question," said my mother, laughing. " The Government itself decides."

" How jolly unfair."

" Well, put like that it does sound unfair," said my father. " And of course it often is. The Messenger tries to publicies cases where people are trampled on unnecessarily; it's the sort of thing Mike Spillergun ridicules so well in his column. All the same, there are times when the Government, or the local authority, *have* to be ruthless—for everyone's sake. That's what they are elected for. Besides, anyone who feels he has been unjustly treated has several legal means of redress."

" Everyone *always* feels he has been unjustly treated—it's human nature," said my mother.

" Not necessarily. The Government can be over generous on occasions, as well as too stingy. Plenty of speculators made fortunes in the war selling land they'd bought cheap to the Government at a profit—Sprockett started his career like that with Dippenfield Aerodrome, you may remember."

" Well, supposing you owned Cowdray Park and there was a war and they wanted it for a bombing range?" asked Friday. " What would you feel *then*?"

" I really haven't the faintest idea what I'd feel or do," Daddy answered, a trifle huffily. " Luckily the question will never arise."

" Well, I know what *I* would do," I said. " I'd ride a polo pony in the middle of the park and tell them to bomb me and be damned!"

" Steady, Gus. Fitchetts is the next entrance on the left— where that car's turning." My mother again drew in her breath and pressed on the floor. The tense moment over, Daddy teased Friday by saying: " *How* I'm looking forward to meeting the great P. Blow! Rather odd if he *is* Jasper Blow's son, all the same," he added thoughtfully.

" Don't expect me to ask him," said Friday.

An avenue of beeches overhung the drive. I remembered how Gail and I had schooled our ponies in and out of the trees riding to our first meet. " It's freezing hard," said my father, as if aware of my thoughts. "I rather doubt if you'll hunt to-morrow."

Our headlights lit up the back of the car in front.

"I think that's the Sprocketts," my mother said. " So at least we'll know someone. Perhaps they've brought Helen, Feb."

My father, who detests the Sprocketts, groaned. My mother and I are rather fond of them, at least of her. She has a good heart underneath all the diamonds and nothing proves it more than that, on my suggestion, she adopted Helen Ponton, an awful girl who went to my school and whom I loathed, but whose parents were killed in an air crash so that she had to spend her hols with a maiden aunt in Leamington Spa. I can't say I liked Helen any better after she came to live with the Sprocketts in Dippenhall. She had been conceited enough as a poor orphan; as the only child of multi-millionaires she became intolerable. However, we seldom met because they took her everywhere on their travels, with a special lady's maid to look after her clothes, and a special governess to teach her French. I had thought the Sprocketts were away for Christmas in Jamaica and I feared that, now they were back, we would have to ask Helen to the dance.

For a moment, following the Rolls down the cavernous drive, I thought again of the letter from the bank. If Daddy really was broke, perhaps the dance would have to be cancelled, so that was something. Might we even—horrors!—have to sell the ponies? Doubtless worse things had happened to girls of my age, but off-hand I couldn't imagine what. At least the ponies couldn't be sold before to-morrow's hunt. Or would the frost prevent hunting?

"Blast," I exclaimed, and then tried to turn it into a sneeze.

"Darling, you've caught a chill and that's why you're looking so off-colour," said my mother. "I knew you shouldn't have come."

"It's not that at all," I muttered furiously.

Our headlights lit up a mass of cars parked on the frosty grass verge. Ahead of us the Rolls drove into the welcoming pool of light at the front door.

"To save your shoes I'll drop you out and rejoin you later. I want to park the car so that we can make a quick getaway." What my father really wanted was to avoid having to meet the Sprocketts.

We followed Lord and Lady Sprockett into the hall. Helen was with them. Without speaking, she and I gave one another a critical once-over, to see which was on top. *She* was easily; indeed, she had changed entirely in the few months since we last met. Her hair, long before, had been cut short and swept up, with a highly artificial effect of casualness, on top of her head. She wore lipstick, high-heeled silver shoes, and a silvery wrap fringed with white fur, which she handed, with a gracious smile, to a maid. Underneath she had on a long-sleeved frock of pale-blue moiré silk and altogether looked about seventeen, instead of not yet fourteen—my age.

"Hallo, February; nice to run into you again," she said distantly, dabbing at her great fat face with a compact, while I gave the maid my old tweed overcoat which had once been Friday's.

"Pretty frock," I commented. My own red velvet dress had belonged to my mother in her youth.

"Oh, *this* old tea-gown. Lelia bought it for me in Paris

last September. It's absurdly *démodé*, of course, but all right for the country. I rather like yours too—velvet has such old-fashioned *ingénue* charm. And doesn't red have some connection with hunting?"

"Not this red."

"You still ride, I suppose?"

"Madly."

"*Toujours le* tomboy . . ."

On the spur of the moment I couldn't think of an answer to that, at least not in French. I just thought of all the trouble I'd taken to help Helen out of her rut in Leamington Spa. . . . I had begun to boil and drifted off towards Friday who, I could tell, was now stretching himself to make the blue suit look smaller. Mummy chatted to Lady Sprockett and I heard the latter say confidentially: "My dear, do point out our hostess when we go in. I don't know her from Moses, do you?"

"I think so, but I've only once met her. Aren't they friends of yours then?"

"Not at all. Can't imagine why we were asked except that I believe he and Ted have had business dealings recently. Some skulduggery or other, I shouldn't be surprised."

"I shouldn't be surprised either," my mother said, smiling.

Lord Sprockett himself ignored us and just stood staring at the decorations, wondering how much they'd cost—or so I guessed.

A deafening party noise of chatter and clinking glasses came through the doors of two large rooms which opened off the hall. Certainly the Gumbles had spared no expense. The hall itself, empty save for the maid who took our coats, was elaborately festooned with every sort of garland, not to mention balloons, holly wreaths and six great suns made out of pleated gold paper.

"We could do with some of all this for the dance," I whispered to Friday.

"The Gumboils must be rolling," he replied.

We followed the Sprockett family into the nearest of the two rooms. It was the drawing-room and decorated on the same lavish lines as the hall, only jammed full with guests, none of whom I knew by sight. As far as I could tell there wasn't a soul of my age present. My mother spotted that too and said in an aside: "This looks as if it might be rather hell for you. But cheer up. Probably wizard grub."

Lord Sprockett, who never had any manners, just elbowed himself into the crowd, leaving us in the doorway.

But at that point our host, who turned out to be the tall man I'd seen on the downs that afternoon, loomed suddenly into view, a head and shoulders above the nearest guests. In my experience there are two sorts of host. The timid type who looks as if he's hating every minute and probably is and who seems to be saying: "I do apologise for having subjected you to this fate worse than death." And the hearty, or Wardle, type. Captain Gumble was that sort. His very moustaches radiated seasonal cheer.

"Lady Sprockett! Mrs. Callendar! Splendid! Well done getting here. Delighted you were able to make it. Come on in, come on in. Splendid!"

The way he greeted them he might have been Sir Edmund Hillary hailing the long-lost Fuchs party at the South Pole. Lady Sprockett allowed him a brief handshake, shuddered slightly, and pushed off in search of champagne. Mummy quickly said: "Your wife kindly asked me to bring our two

eldest. I do hope that's all right?" And she introduced
Friday and me, also Helen who had been left stranded by her
adopted parents.

"Of course, of course. Delighted! Splendid!"

Captain Gumble, who didn't recognise me, bent down and
breathed Christmas spirit, or at any rate spirit, on us, saying:
"I'll get my young nephew Peter to cope."

"Peter!" he shouted over his shoulder, with slight exasperation, I thought. "*More* of your guests. Come and do your
stuff."

Then he led Mummy off. "So glad we've met at last. I
believe you knew my cousin Ernest when he ran a gallery in
Bond Street."

I heard her answer, in her affected party voice. "Oh, but
of *course*. I hadn't realised he was your cousin. . . ."

A tall bored-looking youth, with dank smoothed-back fair
hair and dressed in an immaculate dinner-jacket, now appeared.
Friday contrived to stand immediately behind me while the
youth gave us both a fleeting glance. His glance at Helen was
less fleeting.

"Come and have a drink, won't you?" he said, taking her
by the arm.

She smirked. "That would be most welcome. But nothing
trop fort, please."

They, too, melted into the throng.

"So *that's* P. Blow," I said.

Friday nodded glumly. "That's P. Blow."

"Well, all I can say is I just *pray* he's out hunting to-morrow,
and I get a chance to jump the Grey Arab on to his face."

My father's voice spoke behind us. "You two look as if
you're having the time of your lives. Why not try the other

room? I think I saw Adam and Sasha Henry and a few more of your age. I peeped in there to find my hosts, but they're said to be here. I'd better just say ' Hallo ' and then I'll come and join you."

The other room was a library and had been left bare of decorations. It, too, was pretty full of grown-ups talking their heads off, but at least there were some younger guests including Dr. Henry's son and daughter, who are great friends of ours and live between Brampton and Querbury. Sasha's my age and Adam is eighteen, but he's not the sort of boy who lets that make any difference.

" Thanks awfully for asking us to your dance," he said, fetching me an iced orange squash and a plateful of sausage rolls. " Does it matter if I come in this old suit? I'm afraid I don't run to a dinner-jacket."

" Ass," I said, and told him about P. Blow and Helen.

" He must be dotty. You're ten times prettier than that dolled-up slug."

Adam had left school the term before and was thrilled because the local repertory had given him a job as an assistant stage manager, starting with the New Year. We retreated to a quiet corner of the room, so that he could tell me about it.

There was a writing-desk in the corner, obviously tidied up for the party. The papers had been stuffed into pigeon-holes, but a large box file stood on the desk's flap, among ash-trays and glasses. Without particularly meaning to pry into Captain Gumble's affairs, I idly lifted the box's lid while Adam poured out his hopes and ambitions. Apparently, if you worked in rep. in however humble a capacity, you always had the chance of a small part.

" They're doing *Othello* in March and I know the part by

heart. I played it twice at school. If only I can wangle myself as understudy to the present leading man, then maybe . . ."

"Drop a heavy prop on his head just before the curtain goes up," I suggested vaguely. The file contained typed business letters, mostly with the printed heading *The Downland Preservation Company Ltd.* The top letter began: "My dear Jasper," and was signed "Horace Gumble, Capt." But that was all I had time to read.

I closed the lid quickly at the sound of a familiar voice nearby saying: "Got all you want? Splendid, splendid."

Our host pushed his way through the crowd towards where we stood at the desk.

"Here, you two seem to have run out of food and drink.

Go and help yourselves at the table. That's the idea. Splendid."

While Adam grabbed another plateful of sausage rolls I kept an eye on Captain Gumble. He opened the file, thumbed through it, extracted a paper and stuffed it into a pigeon-hole. Then, tucking the whole file under his arm, he strode off into the hall where Lord Sprockett waited. The two men vanished together through another door.

And then I saw my father. He was watching them too, as he pretended to listen to a conversation between two females. Making some excuse, he left his companions and strolled to the desk, where he put down his glass and pulled out a cigarette case. No one, who hadn't been observing carefully, would have detected his next action, so casual did it seem and so quick. His hand shot out and grabbed a paper from one of the pigeon-holes, disappeared with it into his pocket and re-appeared holding merely a box of matches with which he lit his cigarette.

I could hardly believe my eyes. It would be difficult to find a more *honest* person than my father. He gets in a fuss if he owes anyone even a penny, and the idea of him pinching letters off his host's desk was absolutely fantastic. And yet I'd seen it.

" Golly, you old twister," I said—louder than I intended.

" Sorry, there's such a noise I couldn't hear," Adam said politely.

" Oh, nothing. I only asked who's that chap talking to your sister."

" I don't see Sasha anywhere. . . ."

But my father caught sight of me and came across the room. " Ah, there you are. Time we all went home." He looked thoroughly harassed and depressed and never even said " hallo " to Adam, who's his favourite of all our friends.

Ten minutes later, in the car again, my mother said: " Well, that was all great fun. I hope everyone enjoyed it as much as I did. Did you, Feb?"

" It was ghastly."

" Frightful," Friday agreed.

Daddy was silent.

" You *are* hard to please. And by the way, Gus, that boy *is* Jasper Blow's son. Captain Gumble married Jasper Blow's sister. In other words, they're brothers-in-law."

" I learnt that too," he said curtly.

We got home to find a police sergeant standing at the front door, about to push the bell.

" Mr. Callendar?" he inquired in a voice of doom. "I wonder if I could have a word with you?"

My father took him off to his study. Mummy didn't seem worried, but I felt quite faint with anxiety again. I even wondered if Captain Gumble might have phoned the police— but that was absurd. Later I heard the policeman leave, giving a cheerful, " Good night, sir. Sorry to have troubled you."

" That's all right, Sergeant. Glad to help," my father replied.

" What did he want?" Mummy asked, when we were eating a cold snack in the kitchen.

" Oh, just a routine check on something. Too trivial to explain."

He retired to bed early and I'm afraid I soon forgot everything except my own excitement for the next day's hunt.

Chapter 6

As usual my father proved to have been too pessimistic. Thursday dawned brightly and there was no frost that the sun wouldn't clear by 11 a.m. Gail and I were up before light, fetching Gorse and the Grey Arab in to the stables to groom them and give our tack a final polish. Daddy called in for a moment before catching his train. He still looked awfully worried, I thought, but quoted one of his favourite Jorrocks jokes. Personally, mad though I am about hunting, I find all Surtees's books deadly. However, he thinks they are terrific.

" The image of war without its guilt, and only twenty-five per cent of its danger. I've told you that definition of hunting before, haven't I? "

" Only about a hundred and fifty times," I answered, polishing a snaffle.

" Well, enjoy yourselves. It's a great consolation to me, while I work myself towards an early grave, that at least you're all having a super childhood."

" Why work yourself to an early grave then, if you don't feel like it? " I said unsympathetically. " We'll have a super childhood either way. Besides, I'm not a child, I'm a teenager."

But he had already started up the car and didn't hear.

I admit I'm a slut and couldn't care less what I look like in most things, but I wouldn't be seen dead with a shoddy turn-out on horseback in public. I don't mean I want to appear smart particularly. That's a question of lolly—expensive clothes and tack will always beat cheap stuff and mine is mostly cheap stuff. Perhaps *workmanlike* is the word I'm after—everything looking as if it was kept for use, rather than for show, but—and this is the whole point—*well* kept. If I soaped my neck as often and as hard as I soap my saddlery I wouldn't have a neck left, and Mummy often complains that if I took the trouble to tidy my room that I take sweeping the stables and arranging everything there in order, then my room would be a model exhibit in the Ideal Homes Exhibition. Which, thank goodness, it never will be. All of which is simply to say that when we had prepared ourselves and our ponies for the hunt, there was hardly time to swallow a few mouthfuls of cornflakes and pocket a sandwich or two for a snack later, before setting out.

There's a short cut across fields avoiding Brampton, but we preferred to hack all the way to Fitchetts by road, to be sure of arriving clean. My mother tried to persuade Friday to bike to the meet and follow the hunt, but he got out of that by offering to work on the decorations for the dance. Whereas, of course, he merely wanted to avoid meeting P. Blow.

Our lane crosses the Quer near the cottages and as we rode over the little bridge Gail cried: "Look, the swans again."

All seven were drifting downstream in formation, their necks curved proudly at the same angle.. At the sight I involuntarily sat up straighter on the Grey Arab and rode with an extra swagger, like a Lifeguardsman. And why not? No point in not being proud when you're on horseback—it's the proudest thing in the world to be—except perhaps a swan.

"Sit up," I said sharply to Gail. "You're like a sack of potatoes this morning.'

"Don't be so bossy," she said. "And, anyway, who fell off at the Querbury Gymkhana last hols? Not me."

"A good rider needn't be ashamed of falling off. It's often better than clinging on and jabbing the horse in the mouth which was what you did over the brick wall. . . ."

We argued about who was the better rider till we reached Brampton where we intended to buy a few bars of chocolate in the village stores. The store is owned by Mr. Bunn's wife, a dark spiteful little woman with whom we're friendly on the surface, though we suspect that both she and her red-faced farmer husband hate us underneath. She must have made a lot of money from various businesses she owns in Querbury, as well as from the store which has expanded to double its size since we've known it.

Gail held the horses while I went in to get the chocolate. Mrs. Bunn herself wasn't there. I gathered from an assistant that Mr. Bunn would be at the hunt, and that his wife was also going to the meet.

"Quite the fine lady these days, is Elsie Bunn," one woman customer standing nearby said to another. "Doesn't care to be reminded of her own brother even."

"Never knew she had a brother."

"Dark little cockneyfied chap—works for Sprocketts. We saw him in Querbury the other day, remember?"

"Oh, that creature. Fancy him being her brother. . . ."

The assistant, lapping the gossip up maliciously, handed me the chocolate bars and I left.

On the main road we joined a straggling procession of other horsemen. The sheer excitement of hacking to a meet is

unlike anything else I know—perhaps, like Christmas, anticipation is really the best part of hunting; I haven't done enough
to tell. This was the most ideal day you could imagine, with
the sun breaking through a haze and with enough frost on the
ground and hedges to make the whole landscape sparkle. I
felt all keyed up, jumping double-oxers in imagination, row
upon row of them. Squabbling with Gail was just my way of
letting off steam.

" Let's canter down the drive between the trees—give the
ponies a good bending," I cried, as we passed through the
gates.

However, the ground was boggy, with a danger of roots
tripping us, so I jog-trotted between the trees instead, bumping
the saddle and with the stirrup iron on the toe of my boot like
the Household Cavalry in the Mall. A car swept close by,
sending a muddy spray from a puddle all over the grey Arab's
off side, and mine.

" Why can't you look what you're doing," I shouted
furiously, almost in tears. It was the Sprocketts' Rolls and I
caught sight of Helen, in a fur hat, grimacing through the rear
window.

" You . . ." But perhaps I'd better not repeat what I shouted
at her.

Gail, riding up behind, didn't make matters any better by
laughing. My father says that rage is a kind of poison best
worked out of the system quickly. When I caught sight
of P. Blow, all got up in a black coat, top-hat, and white
leathers, flirting with Helen Ponton in a camel-hair coat, I
was in a very poisonous mood indeed.

" Hallo, Feb—you're jolly smart," said a voice at my elbow.
" I say though, what a mess your right side is in." Adam had

come to follow hounds on a bike and really I was glad to see him, but just then I couldn't feel friendly towards anyone.

"No need to draw attention to it like that," I snapped. Looking rather hurt, he pushed off again.

The Q.V.H. is a small hunt—we seldom get a field of more than forty, often much less. To-day there must have been about fifty riders and a crowd, double that in number, of hangers-on. I saw Mrs. Bunn in the distance, standing on her own and looking merely spiteful. Mr. Bunn, very smartly turned out on a brown cob, didn't seem to have anyone to talk to either, though he grinned around him, taking off his top-hat to everyone he could. He's a hopeless horseman but, to give him his due, goes hard.

I recognised a few friends of my age—mostly from the Pilchers' riding school in Querbury—but rather avoided them, keeping the Grey Arab on the edge of the throng. He was restive and no wonder. He didn't like being seen at the meet splashed with mud any more than I did. Captain Gumble himself, in pink and mounted on a bay the size, and shape, of an elephant, sat chatting nearby to Lord Sprockett, who was on foot.

"Well, that's all fixed. So glad you agree," I heard him say. "I was on the blower—ha, ha—to Jasper last night. He just wanted to make sure you had no objections. They'll start on Monday week."

Lord Sprockett, puffing at a cigar and sipping a glass of cherry brandy, nodded and said: "Insurance O.K.?"

But I didn't pay much attention to them. I was watching to see what P. Blow would ride and I recognised his mount at once—a large and vicious liver-chestnut called Saladhin,

belonging to the Pilchers. Captain Gumble must have hired it
for his nephew. The horse bucks, can jump anything, has a
mouth of iron and is inclined to kick. It's not everyone who
can manage him. However, P. Blow got up with apparent
unconcern and settled himself, while continuing his conversation with Helen. I flatter myself that I can tell a good rider at
a glance. P. Blow, I had to admit disgustedly, was almost
certainly a good rider. When, two seconds later, Saladhin
gave his famous impersonation of a bronco with a nettle under
his tail, scattering all and sundry, I had hopes. But they were
dashed. P. Blow's seat didn't shift an inch. And, what
annoyed me still more, he kept his temper with the horse,

patting it on the head like a baby and calming it down. There wasn't much doubt that P. Blow was a very good rider indeed.

"Splendid! Well done, young Peter," Captain Gumble boomed, adding proudly to Lord Sprockett: "Hell of a good lad, my nephew—more or less born in the saddle—fed on mare's milk. . . . If he wasn't going into the Greys, he's the sort of chap you ought to try and nobble for your business."

"Doubt if he has enough brains," Lord Sprockett replied. I could have hugged him.

But hounds were moving off towards a coppice in the park and I followed. Helen Ponton, waving at P. Blow's back view, stood beside a large puddle on the edge of the drive. I trotted straight through it.

"Strewth!" she exclaimed furiously, dabbing at her camel-hair coat with a lace hanky.

"What is Truth?" I said, jesting; but, like Pilate, didn't stay for an answer.

The country near Fitchetts is too wooded for a good hunt—the best hope is for hounds to run north across the Quer and on to the Querbury range of downs. We spent an hour galloping up and down rides and jumping the odd fallen tree. But there were too many riders and hangers-on, and we couldn't escape from each other. Nothing is so annoying as to follow another horse along a muddy ride, getting his mud thrown back in your face! A fox was found, then headed by some chap on a bike—Adam, I suspected—and lost again. The Master, a furious sort of man called General Roper-Bassett, could be heard at intervals growing still more furious.

Gail had joined a group of friends on the Pilchers' ponies, and I lost track of her. I stayed by myself, keeping P. Blow in sight, though he was too busy with Saladhin to be aware of me. I had to admit he was a real horseman; someone who tried to understand his mount rather than simply to control it—which he managed easily enough. Once, in a large clearing in the forest, I noticed him actually schooling the horse in and out of the trees and getting him to change feet, something no one had probably tried on Saladhin for years. Then, without effort, he popped him over a large fallen tree-trunk, making a fuss of him all the while.

At one point most of the field seemed to have lost interest and clustered in a ride, smoking and gossiping. Half a dozen of us, including P. Blow and myself, decided to leave the wood through a gate and make our way round the edge to where we thought hounds might break cover if they found—though the hounds, too, sounded dispirited. I was the last through, following P. Blow, who held the gate for me a moment. As I grabbed it from him, Saladhin let fly at the Grey Arab, missing his hock by a hairbreadth.

"Control your horse properly, can't you?" I snapped ungraciously.

But P. Blow simply replied, with extreme politeness and as though he meant it: "I *am* so sorry. You're Friday Callendar's young sister, aren't you? I think we met for a moment last night. . . ."

Before I could answer, the huntsman's horn rang out a hundred yards away outside the wood and the hounds, at the same instant, changed their note to that deeper baying chorus which means business. The real hunt had started.

P. Blow vanished on Saladhin. I was still holding the gate when I heard a familiar voice shout: "Keep it open, that's the girl. Splendid!" The rest of the field, including Captain Gumble, careered towards me down the ride. I tried to hold the gate, but the Grey Arab decided otherwise, and giving a mighty snort set off after Saladhin. The gate, a heavy one with an awkward latch, swung back and shut with a clang. For a second or two I was aware of loud curses aimed at me from its far side. Then I forgot everything in the madness of the chase.

It's in the nature of horsy people to pretend to be more knowledgeable than they are, but I confess I never have the faintest idea what's happening most of the time at a hunt— how hounds are working, what the huntsman is doing with them, why the fox runs in one direction rather than another. In short I don't dig the finer points. To me the whole thing is just a glorious helter-skelter to try to keep somewhere near the front. Would it be as much fun if the fox could somehow be made of rubber? No, of course it wouldn't. Because the desire to *kill* is at the back of it all and you've got to be honest about that, however much you hope, as I always do, that the fox will escape. Still, the helter-skelter is the part I enjoy best.

On this run I had a better start than most. By letting go of the gate, I'd bottled them up in the wood for a vital minute— in which time those of us already outside covered nearly half a mile. The hounds ran straight after a young dog fox. The poor devil (so I heard someone say later) didn't realise he could have doubled back much more safely to another part of the forest. Instead he set off uphill across open fields, with little cover unless he climbed them and descended beyond to the Quer Valley. For twenty minutes or so we went like fury.

The fences were small or had gaps and for once there was very little wire. The Grey Arab is no great jumper but he can gallop with the best and we overtook several grown-ups. I was too excited to bother whether P. Blow was among them, indeed I'd forgotten him. But a moment came when I found myself alone and with the choice of two possible routes into different fields. Anyone who has hunted knows the sort of predicament—make the wrong choice and you may never catch up again. Then I spotted P. Blow galloping across a grassy field to my right. We scrambled over a bank and gave chase. Probably the Grey Arab remembered that kick and determined to show Saladhin just where he got off. We fairly flew in pursuit and had caught up to within a few yards when the field ended at a stiff hedge with a post-and-rails built in, and ditch on the take-off.

P. Blow, as if undecided whether to attempt it, glanced round, saw us, then went straight ahead—and over, with an inch to spare.

The fence was about two feet higher than the Grey Arab had ever jumped in his life and at any other time I would no more have set him at it than at the moon. But there was still a good deal of poison in me; in him, too, perhaps. He knew he couldn't hope to clear it, so he put on maximum speed and took the top rail on his chest, knocking it into the middle of next week. I don't pretend I sat very *securely* in the saddle throughout that operation but at least I was still on board when we landed on the far side, where P. Blow had reined up to see if we were all right.

"Engine trouble?" I asked, as we flashed by—and again didn't wait for an answer.

A minute more and we reached the hilltop. Hounds had checked. The master was there and perhaps half a dozen others all congratulating each other. With the Q.V.H. a clear run for twenty minutes is almost a record. We waited while Jim the huntsman tried a cast round the edge of a spinney.

The rest of the field began to arrive, including Captain Gumble, who came puffing up on his elephant.

"That was a bit of all right, wasn't it?" General Roper-Bassett shouted heartily to him. To which he answered sourly, obviously intending me to hear: "Missed it. A blasted girl slammed a gate in my face."

However, I just gazed in an aloof sort of way across the Quer Valley spread out below us and towards the Querbury range of downs which now filled the skyline to our north. Marsh Manor itself was miles to the east, but you could see the Beacon clump above it.

"I hear this new road is coming slap through you in Querbury," the Master said to Captain Gumble. "Where's it to go exactly?"

But the hounds gave cry and we were off again.

The next hour was more typical of Q.V.H. form. We messed about in and out of woods, working slowly downhill all the time and getting mixed up with bicyclists and cars in a lane. . . .

"They're still on to the same fox," someone said.

"Nonsense," someone else said sarcastically. "They lost *him* hours ago. This is a rabbit. . . ."

Gail, with her Pilcher crowd, joined up and she rode across to me. "We've had a super time. I've jumped *ten* logs."

"Good lord—*logs*," I said. "*I* jumped the moon."

I munched my sandwiches, listening to the Master discuss the prospects with Mr. Bunn, who looked mighty pleased to be consulted. He said he thought our fox had gone to earth ages before and that the hounds, who at any rate appeared to be hunting *something*, might be on to a fresh one.

"The wind's in the west," Mr. Bunn said knowledgeably,

" so he'll run *down* the valley. Never known one run *up*stream, not when the wind's *west*."

I had a feeling he was simply making it all up, but the Master seemed impressed, and said: " Thanks awfully. In that case I'll tell Jim to try a cast *down*wind."

Everyone knows General Roper-Bassett knows nothing about hunting, but he's rich and he likes being the M.F.H., and, anyway, no one else is prepared to devote the time. He galloped off to give his instructions to Jim, but never did, because his horse put a foot in a drain and he went for six. Which was probably all for the best, because Jim, on his own initiative, made a cast *up*wind; the hounds immediately found and ran *up*stream, though whether the fox was the original or a new one, I never learnt.

But what fun we had! There's a wide belt of meadowland along the Quer on the south and for an hour we galloped about there, with occasional darts into fields and woods on the hillside. I was up in front for a while, then I got lost, then hounds doubled back and I found myself near the front again, one of the leading three or four including Captain Gumble, Mr. Bunn, P. Blow and, of course, Jim the huntsman—it always amazes me how Jim is always in front without apparent effort!

We were working along the river's bank, with the hounds two hundred yards ahead, when I saw the fox. He had crossed the Quer and was streaking up on to the downs. I'm never quite sure what you're supposed to shout when you see the fox, but I am sure it's not "Tally-ho!" except in books. Anyway, I cried out: "Look! There he is! How lovely!"

But Jim had already seen him. Calling the hounds, he rode straight into the river, across and up the far side. The water was up to his waist in the middle, but he didn't bother.

"No need to get wet," Captain Gumble shouted. " We can jump it farther on, I know the place." And he galloped off, with us following, while the hounds and Jim disappeared fast on to the downs.

"Damn. The bank's fallen in. Not as narrow as I'd thought. Might be easier to wade after all," Captain Gumble said when we reached his place, spurring his mount into the stream. But the elephant had other ideas. He stopped right in the centre; then, quite slowly, took a swim. Captain Gumble submerged in a torrent of threats and rude words. . . .

I happened to notice Mr. Bunn and I've never seen such an expression of pure joy on a face before. However, he and another grown-up dismounted to lend a hand, but that was no concern of mine. I galloped on and came to a small island, five or six yards wide, which divided the Quer into two streams, each about twelve feet across. If the Grey Arab went at it fast we *might* get on to the island and off again. P. Blow came up behind me—he couldn't be bothered with his uncle either.

"This is O.K.," he said, showing Saladhin the obstacle, before taking him back for a good run at it.

" *I'll* show you the way," I cried, giving the Grey Arab less of a run, in my determination to be first over. So that P. Blow and I galloped at the river almost knee to knee.

We landed safely on the island and I do believe we'd have made the second half as well—if seven swans had not risen suddenly before us on the water, hissing furiously and flapping off downstream. All that happened in a split second. The next thing I knew I was on my head in the mud, at the bottom of the icy Quer.

When, in due course, I had spat out a gallon of Quer and

had partially recovered my wits, I stood neck-high in the stream. I found P. Blow choking and spluttering there beside me. Our horses had remained on the little island and showed some impatience to leave.

We hastily got hold of them again and after ten minutes more of scrambling and splashing, and another immersion or two, managed to lead them across to the north bank. There we both remounted and looked around. The whole landscape was as empty of hounds and riders as a desert.

"I suppose this is really rather funny," said P. Blow.

"I wish I had your sense of humour then," I said.

He began to laugh in a queer way which made me glance quickly at him. His hat, of course, had gone in the river. He was deathly white and blood trickled down the left side of his face. Next he closed his eyes, leant forward in the saddle and toppled on to the ground with one foot still held by the stirrup.

I grabbed Saladhin's reins, before dismounting myself. Then I pulled P. Blow's boot from the iron. I remember wondering if he was dead and if so what I should do next.

"Are you dead?" I asked; somewhat fatuously I agree. But evidently he wasn't, because after a minute he groaned and sat up, in a dazed condition. His face now seemed to be *pouring* blood.

"I'm all right—must have passed out. Sorry," he mumbled.

"You've cut an artery, I think. We learnt about it in a first-aid lecture at school once. I'm supposed to apply a turn-key or you'll bleed to death only I've forgotten where to apply it."

"Then I'll just have to bleed to death," P. Blow said, grinning faintly. He certainly had a terrific sense of humour.

"On second thoughts it can't be an artery because that's

bright red and comes out in squirts. Your blood is mud colour and running steadily. It must be a vein. I'll tie it up with my shirt, if I can tear some off."

Some day you must try tearing a bit off your shirt, while you hold on to two fretful horses, and tying it round the bleeding head of a youth sitting on the ground. It's jolly difficult. I did it.

" Thanks awfully," P. Blow said. " Actually, there's a small flask of brandy in a wallet on my saddle. You couldn't reach it, could you ? "

I did that too. I'd begun to wonder if I wouldn't make rather a good hospital nurse when I grew up, instead of a riding instructor. We both took a swig at the brandy and felt much better.

" Is there a farm anywhere ? " he asked. " Perhaps I could phone. I don't think I could manage to cross the river again, to get back to Fitchetts."

There wasn't a farm. " Look," I said, rather enjoying taking charge of the situation, " we live about a mile from here. You lie still and I'll ride off home with the horses and fetch help."

" No. I'm feeling better now. I'll ride slowly with you, if you'll give me a leg up."

I helped him mount Saladhin and after another swig at the brandy he became chatty as we rode along. He told me he had often stayed with the Gumbles when they lived in Querbury.

" Your uncle's quite a big shot—on the Council and all that."

" Yes. Or thinks he is." He didn't seem too enthusiastic about his uncle, but he was fond of his aunt. " We used to live in Norfolk, but my father's so busy nowadays in London we've moved there. He really only lives for his job."

" He's Minister of Roads or something, isn't he ? "

" Yup." He didn't sound all that enthusiastic about his father either, so I couldn't resist asking if he knew what Mike Spillergun always called him. But he just laughed.

" You mean Blow-your-own-trumpet? Oh, yes. I think it's rather an apt nickname, actually, though my father was furious at first. Now he's got used to it. Politicians have to. Besides, it's better to be lampooned than to be merely ignored."

" My father says at least he's getting a move on with new roads at last," I said. " There's to be one round here, I've heard."

" Yes, there is, actually." He was a great one for "actually."

" Where's it to go exactly—or don't you know ? "

" Actually, I do, more or less. My uncle was talking to my father about it last night on the phone. But I think the details aren't supposed to be public yet."

" Oh, come on," I said impatiently. " I won't tell a soul. And after all, I did save your life ! "

" Well, I suppose it doesn't matter—anyway, it will be in the papers soon. But promise to keep it to yourself. It starts north of Querbury and goes right across the downs. My uncle's rather worried, actually. Like my father, he's all in favour of the road, in fact I believe the whole thing was his idea in the first place, but he's afraid there will be a good deal of local opposition. . . ."

" I saw him up behind the quarry yesterday . . ." I began. And then an appalling thought struck me. I almost fell off, but recovered myself.

" Wait a minute. Across the downs . . . You mean down this valley? "

" Yes, but fairly high up. And, you know, people will say it's spoiling the view or their farmland. . . ."

" But did your uncle mention any names of places— Brampton, for instance? "

" No, it will miss Brampton. He did mention somewhere —one of the places he was particularly worried about. I can't remember the name, except that it sounded soggy."

I said nothing, my brain in turmoil. And then : " Soggy . . . Marsh Manor, perhaps? " in a very quiet voice.

" Yes, that was it. Marsh Manor. Do you know it? Is there likely to be much opposition? "

" There certainly is—from *me*," I said.

Chapter 7

"I DON'T SEE that it's all *that* tragic," Friday said. "A trunk road by the quarry, with thousands of cars whizzing past all day, might be rather fun—liven the place up a bit."

"You're a fool," I retorted angrily.

We sat in my bedroom later that night, discussing the ghastly news—at least I thought it was ghastly. I'd kept my promise not to mention the road to anyone, but I just had to tell Friday. Mrs. Gumble, a rather smart but pointless sort of woman, had fetched P. Blow some hours before and I'd shoved Saladhin in the stable for the night. I didn't trust him not to kick the others if he went in the paddock. Captain Gumble was to send a horse-box in the morning.

"Well, I can see it may stop you riding up to Querbury Beacon. But perhaps they'll build a fly-over, if we make enough fuss."

I hadn't thought of not being able to ride freely on to the downs—that was a further bombshell.

"It's not just riding," I said. "It's the whole idea—a road —a trunk road—here—in *our* valley. Thousands of ugly people dropping ice-cream cartons in the paddock. Endless noise. Shattered peace. And *Querbury Beacon*—the best place left in the South of England. Oh, can't you *see* what it's going to be like?"

Obviously he couldn't see.

" I suppose we might make our fortune running a snack-bar or petrol station . . ." he suggested lamely.

Hell hath no fury like a woman's scorn. My whole scorn was now switched on to Friday, and he slunk off to bed.

I lay awake late, sorting things out.

My father didn't own Marsh Manor, or rather was still buying it on a mortgage and he was nearly 2,000 quid over-drawn as a result of paying his instalments to the Downland Preservation Company. Captain Gumble had something to do with the company as well as being on the Urban District Council. He was all in favour of this new road, but then he would be, being Jasper Blow's brother-in-law. In fact, P. Blow had mentioned it was his idea. My mother called him a real go-getter with a finger in every local pie and Lady Sprockett had talked flippantly about skulduggery—but there was often a lot of truth underneath her flippancy. And underneath Captain Gumble's moustaches and silly-ass heartiness, I had come to suspect there was a pretty calculating mind. In fact, I had come to suspect him thoroughly. The memory of him disappearing on his elephant into the Quer cheered me no end. . . . I hoped he caught a stinking cold.

My difficulty was that I understood grown-ups only too well, but I didn't yet understand their *world*—mortgages and com-panies and overdrafts and things. I needed someone to discuss all this with—a grown-up, outside the family, I could absolutely trust. There was Robin Fawcett of course—but I doubted whether he knew much more about the grown-up world than I did myself—his head was always in the clouds or canal tunnels or somewhere. His father could have helped—the general was a good friend of mine—but too old and aloof.

No, I decided, I couldn't very well pester General Sir Harold Fawcett. . . .

However, the next day provided the perfect answer to my problem.

We spent the Friday cleaning up after hunting. Captain Gumble came himself to collect Saladhin and to thank us for taking care of his nephew. He didn't mention the gate episode. Nor had he caught a cold.

" Young Peter says you were absolutely splendid. Splendid! Ought to be a hospital nurse."

" How's the el—I mean your hunter after his dip? "

" Oh, you saw that, did you? " He glanced suspiciously at me to see if I was pulling his leg, but I can beat anyone at keeping a straight face when I want to; I've had so much practice on the mistresses at school.

" Only from far off," I replied innocently.

" Treacherous place that," he explained to Mummy, ignoring me thereafter. " I must have been mad to attempt it, but you know how reckless one gets . . . in hot blood . . ." To hear him go on he might have charged with the Light Brigade instead of funking getting wet. It was on the tip of my tongue to say that Jim the huntsman had waded his horse across without hesitating, but Mummy cut Captain Gumble short by inviting P. Blow to our dance. " I'll send a card to your wife as a reminder."

At that I slipped off, to tease my brother. I found him in the stables showing Gail how to polish leather properly. He's what's called a fag at Boreham and all he seems to have learnt there so far is how to polish leather. He started to teach me, so I flattened him.

" Good news," I said. " P. Blow is coming to the dance."

He stopped cleaning tack instantly, and went off sulkily to his bedroom.

I forget what happened the rest of the day except that when my father returned that evening he said to Mummy: " Oh, by the way, John Gubbins will be here for lunch on Sunday. He's spending the night and we'll go up on Monday together."

John Gubbins! The ideal person to consult. . . . I thought in bed later. He's the *Messenger* editor and not as old as my father, who once described him as the nicest person in the world. No one understands the grown-up world better than John Gubbins—you need to, to be an editor. If I could only have him alone for an hour. . . . I fell asleep planning some ruse to take him for a walk on Sunday afternoon while my father had a snooze. . . .

I woke in the early hours of Saturday with all the unmistakable signs—I shivered, my nose and eyes felt swollen, my head burned and there seemed to be no blankets on the bed, whereas there were six. I padded out in bare feet to the bathroom and filled a hot-water bottle. As I got back into bed I gave a sneeze that shook Marsh Manor on its foundations. When I woke again at breakfast-time my head was bursting, my eyes and nose streamed, and I shivered so violently that the bed creaked the floorboards and Mummy came upstairs to see what was wrong. In short, it was I, and not Captain Gumble, who had caught the stinker.

There's only one thing to do with a really heavy cold and that's to bury your head under your wing, so to speak, and hibernate. . . . I hibernated for the next thirty-six hours. By Sunday lunch I was worn out but faintly pleased to be still alive. I heard John Gubbins arrive and the sounds of a parti-

cularly hilarious lunch party; he has a marvellous laugh like
twenty whizz-bangs. He whizz-banged away through the
afternoon—it was raining and they all played games in the
living-room. Gail brought me tea and I sent a message to say
I wanted to see John Gubbins very badly, if he was willing to

risk catching his death. But editors are used to taking risks and
a minute later I heard him bounding up the stairs.

"Poor old Feb," he said, giving me a kiss and a hug. "In
trouble as usual. How are you, you little beast?"

That's the sort of person he is. I felt fine, the cold all dried
up of a sudden, and ready to talk my head off. I talked it off,
while he listened—grinning affectionately at first, then growing
increasingly serious.

"Just a moment," he interrupted at one point. "Are you
certain that the letters you saw at the Gumble party were signed
by Captain Gumble himself?"

" Absolutely."

" And that they were on Downland Preservation Company notepaper ? "

" Positively."

"I see." He sat beside of my bed scratching his head which, with John Gubbins, helps his brain to work.

At length he smiled, and said: " Don't worry about your father's overdraft. These vast sums are rarely as serious as they sound. The *Messenger* already owes him almost as much as that —the cheque's on its way. And I don't suppose the policeman business means anything either—probably badgering him to subscribe to the Sports Fund or something. Still, I'd like to know what the paper was Gus pinched off Gumble's desk. . . . And I *am* rather amazed that Gumble signed that letter you saw, addressed to Jasper Blow. You see, I happen to know quite a lot about the Downland Preservation Company. They own miles and miles of land round here—have been buying it up ever since the war, as a speculation."

" What's that ? "

" Oh, buying land and renting it to farmers, or whoever wants it, for the time being, in the hope that some day the value will go soaring up—for instance, for a building estate, or a new town, or even a new road. Then, of course, they sell it again—at a profit. Perhaps an enormous profit."

" That doesn't sound fair."

" Oh, yes, it's quite fair—like buying and selling anything else at a profit."

" Yes, but *land*. Especially the *downs*. They're part of England, they're everybody's, surely a sort of heritage."

" Well, they're especially beautiful, I agree. But then so are, say, many English pictures. They're part of a heritage

too, but no one objects to their being bought and sold at a profit."

I was perplexed and changed the subject. "What's a mortgage? Did the Downland Preservation Company lend Daddy the money for Marsh Manor?"

"Yes. A mortgage is just the name for lending money to buy land; with the land itself as a security till the debt is paid. The D.P.C., as it's usually called, already owned most of the downs round Marsh Manor. Your father couldn't raise the capital and borrowed it from them. I acted as a sort of witness for his good character—that's partly why I know about the D.P.C."

"Why are you so surprised that Captain Gumble wrote those letters? Isn't he anything to do with the D.P.C.?"

John Gubbins scratched his head again. "Not that I was aware. The Managing Director's called Bunthorpe, I've always understood. Gumble has nothing to do with the company at all, at least not as it's registered at Bush House, which all such companies have to be. He's certainly not a director. Of course he may well be a shareholder—that's quite a different matter. I shall try and check that to-morrow."

"Is Lord Sprockett a director?"

"Yes, I believe he is, but the D.P.C. isn't one of his major interests. They got him on to the board a year or two ago when he bought Deans. His name is useful on the notepaper, and, of course, he has a good deal of influence generally. . . ."

There were restive sounds downstairs and I heard Gail shouting: "John, would you like to play charades?"

Blast them. I hadn't asked him half the things I wanted to know and now I couldn't remember what they all were.

"When shall we hear about the road exactly?"

"As a matter of fact Jasper Blow is holding a Press Conference to-morrow afternoon. Perhaps he'll give out details at that. I wouldn't go normally, but I think now I will."

Friday came bursting in. "We're playing charades. You and I and Gail are being the first team, so do buck up. That is . . ." he added more politely, "would you like to play? No *need* to, if you'd rather not, but it will mess up the whole idea if you don't. We've thought of RUSSIA as the word and RUSH is to be in a newspaper office."

"What are you going to do for HER or is it AH?" I asked.

"Neither. ER. John's to be Gail's husband and they're having a row and I'm just a bystander, so I say, ' If I was you, guv, I'd give 'er a good clip on 'er ear.'"

"O.K., I'm coming," John said. "Well, Feb, stay here quietly like a good girl and in about a week I dare say you'll be allowed up for an hour or two."

I just grinned feebly. My nose had begun to swell up once more.

"Do come and see me again before you go," I snuffled through the handkerchief.

But of course he forgot.

Chapter 8

I WAS STILL tottering around, half in bed half out, on Wednesday, when the story of the new trunk road made the headlines. Eventually, I gathered, it would join London to Portsmouth, using the route of existing roads much of the way. Negotiations were still afoot to buy the necessary land. Meanwhile the Government, in the person of the Right Hon. Jasper Blow, P.C., M.P., O.B.E., was going to complete a ten-mile stretch at record speed—and at record expense—to demonstrate how easily we could solve our national traffic problem if we tackled it ruthlessly. Starting from beyond Querbury, this first section was to run straight across the downs westwards. It would be finished by Easter and cost seven million pounds.

" We in Querbury are proud that we shall be the scene of what may become the turning point in the national campaign to solve the traffic problem," Sir Gilbert Crump, M.P., was quoted as saying pompously in an interview.

My father wrote the *Messenger* article on the subject of the road himself and gave us more details that evening when he and my mother sat round the kitchen table over supper with Gail, Friday and me. Of course he was completely caught. For years he'd been advocating a really drastic policy for roads and now that one was to be put more or less through his own garden there was nothing he could do but pretend to shout, "Hooray!"

"Do you know *exactly* where it's going?" Mummy asked, toying with a cold pork chop.

"Only too well. The north carriageway will touch the edge of the quarry, the south will take twenty yards off the top of our paddock."

"Twenty yards off the paddock!" I exclaimed. "But there won't be enough grass left for the animals!"

"Oh, I expect there will be," he said, uncomfortably.

"At least you'll get a whopping lot of compensation, won't you?" Friday asked. "You know, like you told us that evening in the car."

"I would—if it belonged to me. As it is, I'm not sure that it does."

"Because of the mortgage?" I said, forgetting I was not officially supposed to know. But he seemed too utterly tired and wretched to notice the slip.

"In a way. Just before Christmas the mortgagees—that's the company I borrowed the money from to buy Marsh Manor —offered to buy half the paddock back from me at a very fair price. I was hopelessly behind with the payments and I thought they were being rather generous—giving me a chance to clear the debt. . . ."

He glanced at my mother, but she seemed intent stirring a salad dressing.

"You mean you *did* sell them half the paddock and now *they'll* resell to the Government and get the compensation?" Friday asked. He didn't actually say, "You sucker," but that's what his tone of voice implied. My father flushed angrily.

" I agreed to sell—perhaps it was naïve of me, but I never dreamt of the road. I've only discovered since that they already knew."

" Wasn't that rather crooked of them ? "

" Maybe. The whole thing is too involved to explain. Anyway, I'm sick to death of it, so let's not discuss it any more."

" What happens when we want to ride up on to Querbury ? " Gail broke in. " Surely it will be rather dangerous us crossing the road ? "

" You won't be riding up on to Querbury. There will be a continuous fence. To reach the Beacon you would have to go six miles back to Querbury and take the Querbury-Dippenfield road which crosses the new one somewhere by a fly-over. I'm not sure even then how you would get off it on to the downs."

" I don't see why they don't put the road the other side of Querbury Beacon—through Dippenhall," my mother said. " You'd think that was more in the direct line to Portsmouth and it would do far less damage there, except to Lord Sprockett's pheasants."

" That probably answers your question. . . . Lord Sprockett won't have it on his side. . . . Which reminds me, I haven't told you the whole story yet—the underpass idea. They're going to use the canal tunnel ! "

" What ! " we all gasped.

" Yes, the plan is to widen it and make a new secondary road under the downs from Dippenhall, to join the Querbury-Chichester road this side of Brampton. By the way, Jan, you'll be glad to hear they're straightening your corner in Brampton too."

" But the tunnel comes out in our garden!" Gail said.

" So will this road. Oh, it will only be quite a *small* road—just large enough for Sprockett to drive from Dippenhall to his yacht in Chichester Harbour without having to go all the way round by Querbury. At least I shall get paid compensation for that—so that's something. Well, let's get to bed now and snatch a good sleep while we can. The next couple of months are likely to be pretty noisy round here—both night and day. Besides, I'm pooped."

" Poor darling, I'm sure you must be," my mother said, starting to clear up.

Friday was the only one of us who did not feel appalled at the whole prospect. Bulldozers and grabs and cranes and draglines, and above all noise, are the breath of life to him. " To think they'd never have dreamt of the tunnel if *I* hadn't discovered it," he said with obvious satisfaction. None of us had the energy to squash him.

" There's one thing I don't understand," I said, before Daddy left. " The papers say the Government can't build the whole road because they're still negotiating with landowners. How have they been able to get the rest of the land for our stretch so easily ?"

" As it happens, the ten miles round here are all owned by the same company. The D.P.C. has been amazingly lucky—it's selling to the Government at an enormous profit all along the line. Now I really am going to bed. Come on, darling, let's leave the children to wash up. It will be practice for them, for when we open a Petrol Pump and Snack-Bar, which is the only way I can see of yet turning all this disaster to good account."

"I'm all for it," Friday said. "The Callendar Chips and Comfort Station. Can I leave Boreham the minute I'm fifteen?"

"Not only can you. You *will*," my father said savagely, and retired.

In the next few days our thoughts were divided equally between the prospect of the road and the preparations for the dance. A chain-gang of Callendars got busy in the barn with mops and dustpans.

The "mess-room," as it's known, was originally an apple loft. My father, when we moved to Marsh Manor, put in a couple of decent windows, patched the floor and had the rafters covered with plaster board. Three great tie-beams, ideal for hanging lights and decorations, span the ceiling. Friday spent hours climbing about on them like a monkey. He's rather an expert gymnast, as well as a show-off, and took pleasure scaring us, when things grew dull, by standing on his head on the highest beam. The actual scrubbing of the floor was done by Gail, under my supervision. (I would have liked to help her but felt that it would be silly to risk starting my cold up again!) Once she had finished, we french-chalked it and set Berry, Chrys and Des loose sliding up and down. The final polish was given by Hildebrand.

The north window of the mess-room—or dance hall as it might now be called—commands a view of Querbury Beacon. One afternoon we watched several lorry loads of men move slowly across the side of the downs unloading stakes and driving them in—presumably to mark the road's boundaries. On Saturday morning Friday, who had biked in to Querbury to fetch a supply of hundred-watt light bulbs, reported that the

stakes stretched westwards all the way across the downs from the north of the town and that a small convoy of bulldozers and such like had caused a traffic block on the road which leads out of Querbury to Dippenfield. Evidently they were the advance guard of the army about to attack the new road at its eastern end.

" By the way, it was rather funny—I saw Robin Fawcett in Querbury," Friday added.

" Robin! What was he doing? Why didn't he let us know he was coming? "

" I don't know. I didn't speak to him. He flashed past on a scooter in the main street and I waved madly, but he didn't see me—anyway, he took no notice."

" I suppose he was just passing through and hadn't time," my mother said.

Our own squadron of bulldozers moved in to the attack on the Saturday afternoon. My father was still in London, having stayed up there for some party the night before.

From the barn we heard them rumbling up the lane, and we ran down the short flight of stairs. My mother came out of the kitchen for a minute and stood with us in the yard watching them pass by. Then she muttered: " The old order changeth . . ." and returned to the sink.

The machines were painted bright red with SPROCKETTS LTD. in bold black letters on their side.

" Adding insult to injury," I exclaimed.

" Oh well, they're the obvious firm," said Friday. " I mean, they built Dippenfield Aerodrome and as Lord Sprockett himself is on the spot . . . I'm sick of decorating the mess-room. I shall stroll up to the quarry to have a look."

But the machines were only being brought to the scene of

battle, not going into action as yet. A lorry took all the drivers away later.

"Extraordinary just leaving them there unguarded," Friday said at tea. We were all in the kitchen. Mummy had begun to prepare the dining-room to be used for supper at the dance.

"I don't see why," said Gail. "There's not much danger of hooligans damaging a bulldozer! In any case, no one ever goes there at this time of year."

"Hooligans turn up unexpectedly everywhere," my mother said.

At that moment Daddy drove into the yard. To our surprise John Gubbins was with him; also a stranger. The three men came into the kitchen. "I wish you'd use the front door," my mother said crossly to Daddy.

"All right, don't be alarmed. We're not descending on you for dinner," John said. "We just wanted a sniff of country air for an hour or two. Gus is putting us on a train back at seven forty-five."

"Darling, this is Mike Spillergun," my father said. "I don't think you've met before. . . ."

Mike Spillergun's column may or may not be unlike anything else in English journalism—I wouldn't know. Certainly he himself was unlike anyone *I'd* ever met. He was about six feet tall, and as thin as a fishing-rod, but what immediately struck me was his deeply lined and bony face, with its large hooked nose and turned up mouth, which seemed set in a mocking smile except that his eyes contradicted that impression entirely. They were very large, of a strange violet-green colour and somehow full of sadness. His eyes didn't smile at all.

Mummy gave the men a pot of fresh tea. While the rest

of us noisily discussed the dance preparations and the arrival of the bulldozers, Mike Spillergun just sat watching and listening intently, you felt, behind that mocking smile, but saying nothing. Once I found him staring at me. I looked away, then at him again and, as he was still staring, I stared back. He gave me a stage wink—very slowly with his left eye. Then he picked a scone off a plate, threw it up to the ceiling and caught it between his teeth. A couple of convulsions in his mouth and throat and it had vanished.

" Do it again," we all cried. " That was funny."

" I don't really like scones," he said. " No disrespect to Mrs. Callendar's cooking of course. Now if you happened to have a sword—or a gallon of burning paraffin ..."

" Mike began life in a circus ..." John Gubbins said. "Or was it a zoo? I always forget."

" Both. They wheeled me on in a cage labelled ' *Schpiffeler-ghun*. The only one of its kind in captivity.' Children pushed buns through the bars and I did that trick. But one day one of the buns had a stone inside. After that I went steadily down-hill. ... Sword swallowing, being fired out of a cannon, then *into* a cannon ... until I ended up where I am now, writing for the newspapers."

" Gosh, did you really?" Berry asked, wide-eyed.

" Nonsense, of course he didn't," my father said. " Mike's one of the great success stories of our time. He was chauffeur to an American millionaire and started by pinching cigarettes. Then he started pinching the millionaire's wife——"

" I think that's enough," my mother said, smiling. " Why don't you all go and look at the decorations in the barn. Except Feb. You'd better not go out of doors in this cold. You can help me clear up here and then get Hildebrand to bed. In fact, you should really go to bed yourself."

" Oh, *no* ..." I began, but Mike Spillergun interrupted:

" While the others are in the barn I wonder if February could show me round the house? We haven't long and I've heard so much about it, I'd much rather spend the time looking at all your wallpapers and pictures and things. ...." He flashed a smile on my mother which melted her like butter in the sun.

" Oh, of course ... do ..." she said, slightly amazed.

" Lovely. Come on then, February," and, before I had quite realised it, the extraordinary man tucked me under his arm like a mackintosh and carried me out of the kitchen into the hall, where he put me down.

" Sorry," he said. " I know that wasn't very polite. But you and I have things to talk about and there really isn't much time."

He placed one finger against his nose and winked again, like some absurd villain in a Victorian melodrama.

" Where can we go? "

" Well, I suppose my bedroom's the best place. It's on the top floor."

" Right. Race you upstairs."

There are four flights of stairs and he did the lot in about four strides, with me puffing along behind and wondering if I was dreaming. My room is off the landing and I turned on the light.

" Lovely room to have," he said. " And what a lot of rosettes! Did you win them all on the Grey Arab? "

" Some. Mostly on Gorse."

" You see, I've heard a lot about you. Chiefly from Robin Fawcett."

" Oh, do you know Robin? "

" Rather. A great friend of mine. I like to keep in touch with the rising generation. He and some of his beatnik pals run a jazz club in London I often go to. I saw him a night or two ago."

" Robin's hopeless on the guitar."

" Doesn't stop him playing it! "

He grinned, shut the door behind us conspiratorially and became quite a different person again, a very serious-looking journalist who, you'd have thought, had never laughed in his life. He sat on the chair by the bed and I squatted on the bed itself.

"Now," he said. "First I want you to tell me *everything* you told John Gubbins the other day and anything else you can think of to do with your father's mortgage and the Downland Preservation Company and the new road. Then I shall ask you questions. Shoot. . . ."

I shot.

An hour later my mother shouted from the stairs outside: "February, are you up there?"

Mike Spillergun, with the agility of a cat, strode across to the door and popped his head out.

"Terribly sorry if I've kept her up, Mrs. Callendar. I'm being an abominable visitor. Might I just have two minutes more? We're having a fascinating discussion on the psychology of teenagers—stuff for my column!"

"Not more than two minutes, please," I heard her reply rather crossly. "Gus says you ought to leave for the station and she's had this cold, you see, and should really be in bed. . . ."

"Two minutes dead. I'll be right down."

"Well, thanks, February," he said, coming back. He stood looking seriously at me where I lay curled up on the bed. "There's going to be just the biggest almighty rumpus in a day or two and I'm hoping to keep you and your family right out of it if I can, but I'm afraid I can't promise."

"Oh, I don't care. I should enjoy it."

"I believe you would, too. But your father wouldn't. He's not prepared to lift a finger to help himself in this battle as you know. Give me or John a ring if anything else crops up before Monday night, if you can. You've got the number."

The past hour had been thrilling but exhausting. I had begun to droop with sleep. "I'm afraid they'll start bulldozing on Monday in any case," I said.

"I suppose so. You never can tell. By the way, I've invited myself to your dance next Wednesday, if I can get my Thursday column written early and take the evening off. If you like I'll do my sword-swallowing act as a cabaret turn."

I yawned. "With luck we'll have to cancel it."

"Of course you won't. So be a good girl now and get tucked up under your coverley and I'll dance Sir Roger de Eiderdown with you."

With that he did a couple of comic pirouettes and left like the wind.

Chapter 9

WHEN, ON SUNDAY MORNING, I turned the tap of my bedroom hand-basin and nothing happened, I knew that the *real* winter had begun in earnest. Several times since the hols started the icy grip had threatened to close and had then withdrawn. But now the yard and paddock were starched stiff and white, and I knew somehow in my bones that there wouldn't be another chance to hunt before returning to school. At the same moment I realised that my cold had at last completely disappeared. It's almost worth having a cold just for that wonderful feeling on the first morning it's over, when you find you can breathe freely once more and know that you probably won't have to go through it all over again for another year—or at any rate for several months. I was so full of beans that I almost forgot my worries and the interview with Mike Spillergun and all *that* portended.

My father and the others were to spend the whole day putting the final touches to the barn, seeing that the gramophone worked properly and that the records were in order, and so forth. He was going to London that evening and staying there till Wednesday afternoon when the caterer was due to arrive with the drinks and grub, so he wanted to be sure everything was prepared beforehand.

It's useless trying to help my father—he prefers to do it all himself. Friday's the same. My mother suggested I could make out a list of ideas for elimination dances, but that was no way to spend an exhilaratingly clear winter morning, so without telling her I strolled off towards the quarry, with the vague idea of visiting the hateful team of waiting bull-dozers.

On the way I called in at the paddock to inspect Jane and the ponies. Their long coats, which seemed to have grown even longer overnight to meet the extra need for warmth, bristled with frost. The Grey Arab, whose coat was less protective, gave me a reproachful look as if to say, "How would *you* like to stay out all night in this?"

"I know. I feel terrible about it," I said, rubbing his nose and giving him one of two apples I'd pinched for myself out of the kitchen. "Frankly, if I had my way, I'd keep you in my bedroom. But my parents have narrow minds and, anyway, as long as you move around all the time, I should think you're probably warmer inside that skin of yours than we are in Marsh Manor with nothing but old-fashioned coal fires."

"How would *you* like to have to move around all the time?" he seemed to answer. So I gave him the other apple and pushed off guiltily towards the quarry.

The dozen odd bulldozers, with their exhaust pipes poking up in the air like chimneys, were parked all anyhow near the pond which was covered with a thin layer of ice. The handle of a large half-submerged saucepan stuck out near the pond's edge. Presumably it had been left by the gipsies sometime. I took hold of the handle and with a crack of splintering ice managed to pull the saucepan out. I was examining the bottom, which was in surprisingly good condition for the gipsies to have abandoned it, when the sound of a voice startled me.

A man was talking loudly—almost declaiming—behind a clump of bushes which grew at the foot of the cliff face. A madman? My heart gave a jump or two. I tiptoed nearer, prepared for instant flight. The voice sounded vaguely familiar and yet strange, as if someone I knew was speaking and holding his nose at the same time. The words also were vaguely familiar.

"... I have done the state some service, and they know't ... mumble mumble ... of one, that lov'd not wisely, but too well ... mumble mumble ..."

Creeping right up to the bush, I saw a bike propped against it. That gave me a clue. Stifling the desire to laugh, I peeped round. Adam stood with his back to me. One hand held a little book, the other he waved in the air, fitting the action to the word. I remembered the speech quite well now—the end of *Othello*—and watched breathlessly while he worked himself into a final passion.

"... drops tears as fast as the Arabian trees their medicinal gum ... their medicinal gum ... damn. .... Oh, yes. .... Set you down this: And say besides ..."

He paused, glanced quickly at the book and continued:

" And say besides that in Aleppo once,
Where a malignant and a turban'd Turk
Beat a Venetian and traduc'd the state,
I took by th' THROAT the circumcised dog,
And smote him—THUS."

Adam pretended to stab himself so violently that he staggered back under the force of the blow and saw me.

" Oh, hallo," he said, looking a bit sheepish.

"I say that was super," I said, trying not to giggle. "I there really a chance you might get the part of Othello?"

"Not really. But I thought I'd be ready, in case."

"How's it going at the rep.?"

"Oh, great fun." He didn't sound awfully enthusiastic.

"What do you do mostly?"

"Mostly I just make tea for the others."

"Why didn't you call in, if you biked past us?"

"Well, I was going to—later. I really came to see how the road was getting on. By the way, your friend Blow was here just now on a horse."

" Did you talk to him? "

" No. He pushed off on to the downs."

" Suppose he was just exercising Saladhin."

" More like an expedition: he carried a large rucksack."

Adam put the book away and pulled out a packet of sandwiches. We shared them.

" I'll tell you a joke I heard at the rep. You know the line, ' Hamlet, I am thy father's ghost ' ? What do you think it is in Dutch? "

" No idea."

" Omlet, ich bin da Poppa Spook! "

Later, the sandwiches finished, he said suddenly: " I say, you must rather hate all this, don't you? "

" I certainly do. Of course Friday thinks it will be fun to watch them working. Do you think they'll be able to work if the frost goes on? "

" I'm afraid that won't hold things up much."

" If we could only hold them up for a day or two . . ." I spoke half to myself, thinking of Mike Spillergun's Tuesday column and wondering if he might succeed in stopping the road altogether.

" Why? " Adam asked sharply. " Does a day here or there really make any difference? "

I was on the brink of being indiscreet, but managed to check myself.

" There's just a *possibility*—I can't explain what it is—that the road might be cancelled, or at least held up till various things have been sorted out. But we shan't know for a day or two. And of course in that time these bulldozers could wreck the face of this hillside for ever! "

" They certainly could. Well, let's hope I'm wrong and

they *are* put off by the frost. Shouldn't you be getting back for your lunch? It's a quarter to one."

" Are you calling in? "

" May I leave it open? I want to run through the whole play again now. It depends on how long that takes."

" I think you're a *marvellous* actor," I said, quite meaning it.

But he just laughed good-naturedly and blushed a little and said: " Well, Abyssinia."

My father left by car for London late on Sunday afternoon, satisfied that the lights, heating, gramophone and the rest were in full working order and that nothing foreseeable *could* go wrong before he returned on Wednesday, unless we managed to burn the place down. He rather enjoys organising these kind of occasions and had even worked out a list of questions for the elimination dances. One such, for the last few couples, was to be, " What is it that has a tail and arms and no legs? "

The answer was a coat.

The next question would then be—and he felt sure this would kill them: " What has legs, but no arms, and flies? " You can guess the answer to that for yourselves.

Nothing more had been said all day about the road; indeed with the general atmosphere of mounting excitement about the dance, the subject was forgotten. We hardly thought of it until ten o'clock next day; that is, on the Monday morning.

Before and during breakfast we had been vaguely aware of activity up at the quarry—spasmodic sounds of engines starting and stopping, a few shouts. . . . After breakfast we were all together in the kitchen, partly washing-up, partly arguing about what time to have a supper break and whether to ask guests to leave their coats in the house *before* crossing to the

barn or whether to make a cloakroom in the passage off the dance room. So that we did not hear the two men approach across the yard until they knocked loudly on the kitchen door.

They were foremen from the bulldozing team. One was a great big red-faced Irishman, the other a little dark cockney who reminded me a little of Mrs. Bunn. Both were almost speechless with anger, both spoke simultaneously and on roughly the same lines.

" If I can lay me hands on the young devil among ye who dunnit I'll twist his insides till they——"

" Just you wait. We've sent for the police. They'll soon sort out the likes of you. . . ."

" Don't you just stand there staring and looking all innocent. I can see yer' all in it together the lot of you. . . ."

" *And* the lady. *You* put 'em up to it. *I* know yer sort— all fancy ways on top and cunning as Satan under it. . . ."

" *Thousands* of pounds this'll cost yer—*thousands* . . ."

" *Millions* more like and don't think yer'll get away with this, because yer won't and what's more, I can tell yer here and now that . . ."

It went on like that for several minutes, with my mother just standing amazed in the open doorway and us crowding behind her and all of us scared silly. What *was* the matter?

" Stop it! Stop it, both of you, *at once*! " she shouted at length, stamping her foot. They stopped.

" I really don't know *what* you're so angry about," she continued. She had begun to tremble herself with rage and shock. " No one here has done anything, that I can assure you. Please say what's the matter. There's a telephone in the house and you're welcome to phone the police this minute. Otherwise I shall."

The cockney remained nasty. " *We've* sent for the police, all right; don't you make no mistake about that. And don't you try kidding *me* you're so innocent. Of course your kids done it. Who else is there round here ? . . ."

" Done *what*? " my mother yelled at him, with such violence that he stepped back a pace, expecting a blow.

The large Irishman took over. " Look, lady," he said, in a quieter voice. " No need to be getting yerself worked up.

It's like this. One of your kids—at least *someone*—filled all the exhausts with water yesterday—the diesel tanks, too, by the look of things. The whole flipping lot's gone west when we started up this morning. Took us an hour before we realised what it was. Those were new machines—special for this job. They've *had* it—see? Take days to repair and it'll cost *thousands* . . ."

" *Millions* more, like," snarled his companion.

" We're responsible, Sid and I; should have left a guard on. But the police said it wasn't necessary and in a place like this, what was the point? How could *we* tell yer had a lot of . . ." He grew excitable again.

" Now, listen," my mother said, recovering her calm. " *No one* here has even *looked* at your machines. Just get that into your heads for a start, will you? Who could have damaged them, I've no idea. If you've really sent for the police, O.K. Otherwise I'll phone for you. The best thing you can do meanwhile is to come in and sit down and wait for them. Or else go back and wait at the quarry. Please yourselves."

The Irishman obviously felt like staying in the warmth of the kitchen—I noticed him glance at the teapot on the table— but his companion was still determined we'd done it.

" You stay here, Paddy; see they don't scarper," he said, spitefully. " I'll get back." And he stumped off across the yard muttering: " *Millions*, that's what it'll cost yer; *millions* . . ."

" Oh, come on in and have a cuppa and cool down," my mother said to the Irishman, which he did.

He remained hostile and suspicious for a bit, but he'd obviously taken a fancy to Mummy and she soothed him further by saying sympathetically: " Look, I'm awfully sorry about this. You know it really wasn't anyone here, I promise you, but I do understand how you must feel. Do the machines belong to Lord Sprockett?"

"Sprockett's the name of the firm. Never heard of a Lord Sprockett. Who's he?"

"Well, he owns the firm—at least, I imagine he does. He happens to live near here. I wonder if I should ring him up?"

"Shouldn't trouble, lady. We got an office, like, in Querbury. We sent one of our chaps back there on a motor bike—to fetch the boss."

"I thought you'd sent for the police," Friday said. Paddy looked embarrassed. "I got sorta carried away, saying that. We sent for the boss first—Captain Gumble. He'll send for the police if needs be."

"Captain Gumble!" I said. "How does he come to be the boss?"

"Don't know *how*, but he's sort of area manager for Sprocketts for these parts—least I've worked for him before on other jobs round here. The Cap'n 'll have something to say about this lot. He can be a proper terror—lose my job likely enough. Not that I care—plenty more going. And of course he'll be well covered by the insurance. But I don't care to see good machinery mucked up like that."

"Of course not," Mummy said, restraining a smile. "We're not exactly delighted to have the road here at all, but we're sorry this has occurred—especially if it will get you into trouble. Are you insured against the delay as well as the damage?"

"Bet your life the Capt'n has fixed all that."

Personally, I couldn't have cared less that it had happened—in fact, I had to stop myself jumping for joy. But my mind was whirling with the news that Gumble was also connected with Sprocketts. That chap certainly did have his fingers in every pie. Well, this time—if I had anything to do with it—his fingers would get well and truly burnt.

Everyone by now was making a fuss of Paddy. Friday began to question him on what *happened* if you poured water into the exhaust of a bulldozer, or the diesel tank—especially before a severe frost. . . .

"It's like this here . . ." Paddy began, scratching a diagram on the kitchen table with a fork. I slipped away.

"Is that the *Messenger*?" I was asking a minute later. "Put me through to Mr. Gubbins, please. He's in a conference? Well then, Mr. Spillergun."

"Mr. Spillergun's engaged on the phone. Will you wait?" said the girl's voice on the *Messenger* switchboard.

"No, cut in on him. Say Miss Callendar wishes to speak to him. It's *urgent* . . ."

There was a pause and I heard her voice repeating the message to Mike on another line.

Then: "I'm putting you through to Mr. Spillergun now. . . ."

Paddy had returned to the quarry and we were settling down to a snack lunch when Captain Gumble himself called in. He had already been to inspect the damage, heard of the visit we'd received and, putting two and two together, had obviously come to smooth things over with my mother.

It wasn't hard to see he was livid with anger, though he pretended to hide the fact from us.

"I happen to be in charge of these chaps for the moment," he explained. "I'm afraid they've been boring you—they were a bit upset, rather naturally, but I do apologise. I've given them a rocket."

"It was a perfectly understandable suspicion," my mother said, not very cordially. "But quite unfounded, I do assure you."

"Of course—the very idea," Captain Gumble protested; looking, all the same, as if in his heart he thought it might be anything but unfounded!

"Is the damage extensive?" my mother asked, while feeding Hildebrand some egg with a teaspoon.

"Tiresome—but we'll get over it."

"Who could have done it? Why not stay and have a quick bite with us?"

"No, thanks—got to get back. No idea. There's a gipsy family around here sometimes. I expect you've seen them. I wouldn't put it past them—except that I doubt if they'd know enough about engines even for that simple trick."

"Most odd," Mummy said, preoccupied with a large quantity of egg which Hildebrand seemed determined to return to the spoon.

"Most. Well, I'm on my way. Just wanted to say how sorry I am about those men being a bore. . . ." He looked round at us all rather desperately, but we just went on munching. "About everything, if it comes to that."

"Oh, quite," my mother said. "Forget it."

"Splendid. Well, good-bye, all."

"G'bye . . ." we grunted.

He left.

Chapter 10

DURING THE AFTERNOON the telephone rang. My mother and Hildebrand were upstairs resting and the others were out in the barn playing records, so I answered it. I hoped it might be Mike Spillergun. In fact, it was my father who sounded pretty het up.

" What's all this about the bulldozers at the quarry being sabotaged? I'm told the late editions have got hold of the story. What on earth's going on?"

I gave him a quick account of the situation.

" Have any of you been monkeying about up there?"

" No."

" Promise?"

" Absolutely. Promise." I thought it best not to mention my visit of the day before.

" Thank God. In that case I can relax and enjoy the joke. What other news? Have the police been round?"

" Not yet—I expect they will."

" When they come, simply tell them the truth. I shall be here at the office till eight, if there's any further trouble . . ."

I'd hardly put down the receiver when the front-door bell rang. A uniformed policeman, whom I recognised as the sergeant who had been that time to see my father, and another man stood outside, and I let them in.

" We were expecting you," I remarked chattily.

" Oh, you were, were you? " the man in plain clothes said nastily—obviously a detective. " Are you February Callendar? I've heard about you." But before I needed to answer that, he asked: " Are your father or mother in? I want a word with them."

At that point Mummy herself came downstairs, stifling a yawn and patting at her hair.

" The coppers are here, about the bulldozers," I said.

The police sergeant grinned. But the plain-clothes man, who had a little moustache and looked like a weasel, said pompously: " I should keep your mouth shut till you're asked if I were you, young woman."

" But then you're not me," I snapped—I disliked him on sight.

The sergeant grinned still more broadly, then put up his hand and wiped the grin off. " Sorry to trouble you, Mrs. Callendar, but could we have a word with you in private? " he said.

" Certainly. Feb, just go and get Hildebrand up, please. He's started to grouch."

Hildebrand was perfectly happy enlarging a hole in the sheet. In fact, there wasn't much of the sheet left and he had begun to unravel the blanket. I dressed him quickly and carried him downstairs, determined not to miss more than I could help of the police. I needn't have worried. The police were in no hurry to leave.

My mother had assured them that we could not possibly have done the damage, but the detective insisted on questioning each of us separately in her presence. Berry, Chrys and Des were ruled out almost at once. Gail hadn't been near the quarry for days and was obviously not the sort of girl to pour water down exhaust pipes. Friday admitted having been to watch the workmen on Saturday afternoon, but that was all he knew. The detective evidently believed him. Then my turn came.

I said at once that I'd been up there on the Sunday morning. My mother looked startled. " But you never told me you went to the quarry yesterday. I thought you were with Daddy and the others in the barn all the time."

" I was at first. Then I got bored and went for a stroll."

" Ah," said the nasty detective. " And will you kindly describe your stroll in detail ? "

I told them how I'd been first to the paddock and then mucked about on the edge of the frozen pond. " There was an old saucepan sticking out from the ice ..." I said casually. And only then did I remember Adam. I'd entirely forgotten meeting him.

" Ah, a saucepan ! " The detective exchanged a glance with the policeman who seemed embarrassed. " Tell us more about the saucepan."

" Well, it was just there ..." My thoughts began to revolve at a dizzy pace. A saucepan offered an easy means of ladling water. After I'd pulled it out anyone—Adam, for instance— might have used it. A yawning chasm of dangers seemed to open in front of me, whatever I said next. I blushed and grew flustered.

" Come on, girl. Tell us the truth. So you took the saucepan ? " the detective said.

" No," I said, lying stupidly without thinking. " I only mentioned it because I remember it was there. After that I strolled around for a bit and came home again."

My mother, who has an uncanny way of knowing when I
lie, stared at me hard but said nothing.

"Wait a moment," the detective interrupted. "You say
you *didn't* touch the saucepan. Let's be quite clear about this."

"No." I can't excuse myself for lying the second time, but
that man annoyed me and I was darned if I was going to let
him catch me out. I glared furiously at him and repeated:
"No, I didn't."

"I see." A faint smile hovered under that little moustache.
He had taken a sheet of paper and ink pad from his pocket.
"May I have your fingerprints?"

"Have you any right to do that?" my mother asked quickly, but he avoided answering the question.

"If your daughter has nothing to hide, then it's in her own interest to let me have them."

"Delighted to give them to you," I said, by now boiling with vexation. "Some day they'll be valuable." And before my mother could object I'd planted both hands on the ink pad and then on to the paper—it was touch and go that I didn't plant them again on the side of his face.

"Thank you," he said dryly. And then: "You know, my girl, you're very foolish to take that attitude with me. Frankly, if I was your father, I'd give you a good hiding."

"Frankly, I can imagine nothing more ghastly than being your daughter," I said, and slammed out of the room.

I ran upstairs and threw myself on the bed, trying to sort things out. Silly of me to tell that beastly detective a lie— but what the hell? . . . Who *could* have sabotaged the bull-dozers? I switched on a little bedside radio Daddy gave me a year or two before when I was laid up after an accident. They were playing an Adam Faith record. Which, in the circumstances, seemed like Fate pointing an accusing finger. . . .

But, no. I felt sure it wasn't Adam Henry. True, I'd told him that an extra day or two's delay *might* make a difference; true, also, that he'd sounded wonderfully ferocious as Othello! But I couldn't imagine him wilfully damaging anyone or any-thing. Who else was there? I doubted whether the gypsy family would take such a risk—they were too likely to be suspected. What about Mr. Bunn? The road would mess up his farmland and he was a hot-tempered sort of man. But

damaging the bulldozers would only hold work up temporarily
—so what was the object?

At that point my speculations were stormily interrupted by
the entry of my mother.

She's tall and thin, with a sweet happy expression most of
the time. Now she looked like an angel of destruction. Crossing
the room like a hurricane she switched off the radio and turned
on me as if she intended to tear me in pieces.

" You crazy blundering idiotic little fool! "

" But . . . what have *I* done? " I protested, sounding guilty
the way you always do when you're not sure what you're
being accused of exactly.

" Why didn't you tell me you'd been to the quarry? I'd
already *promised* them you hadn't. Then you went and denied
touching the saucepan. Your fingerprints are all over it. The
wretched man already had the photos in his pocket. He made
me compare them with yours under a magnifying glass. Even
I could see they were obviously the same—for one thing,
there's that unmistakable scar on your thumb from the time
you fell downstairs."

" If you mean you think I dished the bulldozers, that's
absolutely ridiculous," I said, growing angry myself. " I
wouldn't have the faintest idea about pouring water . . ."

" Of course you didn't pour the water. I know that. But
by lying like that you've as good as confessed. That's all the
police want—someone obvious to pin it on. I've never seen
anyone more obviously guilty—cheeking him made it
worse."

" Apart from the fingerprints I don't see how they can
prove I did it—especially as I didn't," I said uneasily.

" I can't imagine what further proof could be needed.

Besides, it's not you I'm worrying about. You won't get into trouble. Daddy will."

"You mean he might have to pay for the damage?"

"He might easily, I should think—if it came to a court case. But that's not what really matters. Oh, there are other sides . . ."

My mother is incapable of being cross for more than a minute. Now she flopped wearily on the chair, resting her face on her clenched hands.

"As a matter of fact I can prove I didn't do it . . ." I began, thinking of Adam; then checked myself. That would throw suspicion on him. Supposing his fingerprints were also on the saucepan. . . . But she wasn't attending.

"Daddy's in a *frightfully* vulnerable position over all this," she said, thinking aloud rather than speaking to me. "In a whole lot of ways. For one thing, when that police sergeant came here a week or two ago he was sent to ask whether Daddy thought the bulldozers could be safely left for a week-end."

"I remember. Daddy was particularly depressed that evening, afterwards."

"Yes, he'd just heard about the road. Anyway, he told the policeman most emphatically there wasn't the slightest risk. Now it looks as if he might have put you up to it."

"Well, really! No one who knows Daddy at all would imagine——"

"You'd be surprised what people imagine—particularly about someone at all well known. They just love to see public figures made to look foolish. It's human nature, I suppose—if not human nature at its most attractive. For instance, years ago—almost before you were born—a famous philosopher and B.B.C. personality was found travelling without the right train ticket. He lost his head and lied and was caught out. Of course it was silly of him. But to hear the whoops of sheer malicious joy which greeted his public humiliation you'd think he was an enemy of mankind instead of someone who had made a valuable contribution to the life of his time."

" Daddy's not as famous as all that surely."

" No, but famous enough for this story to do him a lot of damage if it gets out—and I wouldn't put it past that detective to let it out. Everyone knows Daddy's theories about trunk roads. Several papers have already asked gleefully how he likes having one at his own back door. Now his own daughter is caught damaging the bulldozers. It's a gift—and however untrue it may be people will say——"

" Who cares what people say! "

" Only a fool doesn't care. Oh, Daddy doesn't mind people disagreeing with his opinions. In fact, he often hopes they will disagree—he wants them to argue and discuss things. But he'd just hate them to think him capable of a silly pointless vindictive action of this sort. Besides, there's much more than that . . . I can't explain. I don't really understand it . . ."

" To do with the mortgage ? "

" What do you know about that? "

" Well, at supper the other night he told us the Downland Preservation Company had tried to buy half the paddock when they knew, and he didn't, that the road was planned. So they could sell it again to the Government. . . ."

My mother sighed. " Yes, I'm afraid he's a child in money matters. He's so honest himself he never imagines anyone else is up to something fishy."

Remembering how I'd seen him pinch that paper off Captain Gumble's desk it occurred to me that perhaps my father was less honest than she supposed! However, I simply said, with feigned innocence, " You think there *is* something fishy about the way this road has been rushed through?"

" I do rather. I don't quite know why. So does Daddy. But—because he's the sort of person he is—he can't raise a finger in protest."

" Do you think he should?"

" Oh, women are different—they're not concerned with high moral principles. They just fight if their happiness is threatened!"

" But you think he *should* fight? Or at least *someone* should?" I repeated eagerly.

" *I'd* fight, if I knew how," she said, smiling. And a great relief it was to see her smile. " But all the same, I think he's right not to. I mean, he'd look a hypocrite, after all he's written. And, of course, if the police accuse his family of tampering with the bulldozers he'll look foolish as well. Which is why I got so angry. Oh, dear . . ." She stooped and gave me a kiss. " I'm sorry, darling. You weren't to blame. You lost your head. Well, let's pray the police don't pass the story on to the papers, till they've more evidence. . . ."

Unfortunately they did. Or someone did.

Chapter 11

FROM WATCHING FILMS and the telly I've always imagined reporters are tough chain-smoking types with turned-up macs and turned-down felt hats who say things like, " Make it snappy, kid. We gotta deadline to beat." They're not like that at all, except maybe tough. Mostly they are shy well-spoken characters and have high ideals and were in the "A" stream at school and intend shortly to become editor of *The Times* and meanwhile have convinced themselves they have a responsibility to the public. So that it comes as a real shock afterwards to find they've misrepresented every blessed thing you innocently told them. " If you can bear to hear the truth you've spoken, twisted by knaves to make a trap for fools ..." as someone or other said.

The first of the reporters arrived that same afternoon just before dark.

My mother and I were in the kitchen preparing tea, helped —or rather hindered—by the four youngest. After the police left, Friday and Gail had rushed up to the quarry to see what was happening. When we heard a repeated knock on the kitchen door we thought they'd returned and were trying to be funny.

" Oh, come off it. We know it's only you two clots," I shouted.

The knocking went on, so I tiptoed across the floor, quietly lifted the latch, opened the door suddenly and shouted: " Boo! Bet that scared you!"

"It certainly did," said a nice young man, plump and with curly dark hair. However, he looked more frozen than scared. We asked him in for tea and he told us he was what's called a "stringer"—that is, he had a job on the *Querbury Advertiser*, but also reported for one of the largest, and nastiest, of the London dailies if something cropped up locally. They had phoned him and told him to get a story about—me!

My mother was pretty sharp with him at first. " Doesn't it sometimes make you feel rather ashamed having to go round prying into unfortunate people's affairs?" she asked, putting sugar in his tea.

" Well, of course, I do often get asked that question, Mrs. Callendar," he answered very politely. "I think you should perhaps try and see it from this angle . . ." And he told us how he himself deplored unnecessary prying and would certainly put a stop to it when he became editor of *The Times*, but that meanwhile any self-respecting reporter had a responsibility towards the public at large. . . .

But he hadn't finished explaining all his ideals when five or six more reporters drove into the yard. They were from different London papers and had all shared a taxi from Querbury Station. The taxi waited.

" This is intolerable," my mother said to them in the doorway. " But I suppose you'd better come in now you're here."

They, too, were very friendly and polite—full of apologies for calling at an inconvenient time. They all took sugar with their tea and one made immediate friends with Hildebrand by balancing a spoon on his—that is, the reporter's—nose.

Another of them had a camera and said he was from a Press
Agency. He asked if Mummy would like a snap of the family
having tea. She never can resist snaps of us children so she

agreed and he promised to send her a copy. After that we all
talked a bit about the quarry and how mysterious the damage
was. Then we had quite an interesting discussion about the
responsibility of newspapers to the public at large, and about
something I never understand called Ethics and how the present-
day level of reporting requires, as never before, "A" level in

at least three subjects and, of course, a wide human understanding.

"I hope you will allow me to say, February, how *well* I can understand your feelings about this road and the desecration, as it must seem to you, of the heritage of our beautiful English countryside," said a spectacled youth with a face like a fair-haired tortoise.

"Come again," I said, a bit nonplussed.

"Cyril just meant—and I do so agree with him—that you're your father's daughter," said another one. "We all have a great respect for your father, you know—he's a man of ideals and he's prepared to fight for them. So are you, aren't you?"

"Well, I think you've got to fight some time about something, I suppose . . ." I wasn't too sure what they were getting at.

"The foundations of democracy," said a third, scribbling on a pad. "Too many people nowadays take everything lying down—no initiative any more."

"Wait a moment," my mother interrupted. "If you're suggesting my daughter had anything to do with——"

"Of course we're not suggesting anything of the sort, Mrs. Callendar," several answered together. "We appreciate the situation most sincerely, we assure you. She's a very plucky young woman; wish there were more like her."

I think, though, I can't swear to this, that the blond tortoise had actually mentioned Joan of Arc, when the door burst open and Friday and Gail barged in, saying: "You'll never guess who's working with the team up at the quarry——"

Friday stopped in his tracks. "Gosh. Hallo. Has there been a murder or something?"

"The Gentlemen of the Press . . ." said Mummy.

"Gosh! Reporters! Have they come to hear how old Feb bashed the bulldozers?"

"Don't be an ass," I said hastily.

"Well, we must be on our way," said the Gentlemen of the Press in unison and prepared to leave. Then they thanked my mother most politely for her hospitality, repeated the promise to send the snaps and left. The stringer turned in the doorway, gave me a thumbs-up sign and said: "Attagirl!"

"Who *is* working up at the quarry? You started to tell us . . ." I asked Friday when life had returned to normal—or as normal as it ever is in our household.

"Robin! He's taken on a temporary job with Sprocketts. He's a complete beatnik to look at and there are several others like that with him."

"Did you talk to him?"

"Only for a minute. He gets paid twenty quid a week, he said. He didn't seem very glad to see us, but, of course, he was busy on the job. Twelve new machines arrived on trailers while we were there. The trailers are taking back the broken ones. Robin was helping load them."

"Captain Gumble was there too," said Gail. "Also that boxer. You remember, Feb, the one we saw that afternoon."

"Yup. I remember."

"Actually, the Gumboil was rather rude to us," said Friday. "He shouted, 'You children are in the way. Buzz off. And I'd better warn you there'll be a guard on here to-night—including this dog. *And* he bites.'"

"It's not only his dog that can bite," I said.

Hildebrand, over excited by his contact with the Press, took longer than usual to get to bed. I settled him at last by tucking him up with a spoon. Berry, Chrys and Des are supposed to put themselves to bed—which means they mess about for hours in the bathroom while my mother tidies up their clothes and shouts: " Come along—only a minute more." While this was going on Friday, who never does help with the little ones, popped over to the barn to play through records and Gail went with him—she seemed to have lost her strong sense of family responsibility. I can cope with Hildebrand and up to a point with Des, but the other two refuse to obey me, so I left my mother settling them and went down to the study to search for a good book. I hadn't been in there since the Fifth Day of Christmas and my father's desk still looked in the same chaotic state.

I wouldn't dream of snooping in his correspondence, but I don't count reading letters which happen to be lying on top. One such was a carbon copy of a letter he had typed to the Downland Preservation Company at 3 Sheep's Hatch, Querbury. It was dated 29th December. Apparently he had written it after returning from the Gumbles' party when he knew about the road. It was a short snappy note saying that he had after all decided *not* to sell half the paddock, that he would be obliged, therefore, if the D.P.C. would regard his previous letter of 21st December accepting their generous offer as null and void and that he returned their cheque for £800 herewith.

The telephone rang. There's an extension in the study and I lifted the receiver as my mother answered it in the hall. Daddy was on the line.

She told him about the police and reporters, but evidently thought it best not to worry him by mentioning the fingerprints on the saucepan.

"What did the reporters want? Checking up on the quarry business?" he asked.

"I suppose so. There was nothing we could tell them. We just chatted affably on general topics."

"Um. Doesn't sound like their usual form. Well, we'll soon know. Friday might bike into Brampton early to-morrow and buy the papers in case there's anything."

"Is the *Messenger* printing a story about the quarry? They didn't send a reporter."

"Not as far as I know. John's been rather cagey about the road all day. I have an idea he and Mike Spillergun have been hatching something but I've kept out of it—for obvious reasons. Mike's column comes out to-morrow of course. Everything still in order for the dance?"

"Ah, yes." She sighed. "Except that I wish we'd never had the wretched idea. . . ."

I cut in on the conversation. "Just what *I've* always said. Let's cancel it."

"Oh, you're there, are you?" said my father. "What are you doing in my study?"

"Just borrowing a book when the phone rang."

"Have you any idea who *might* have done the damage?"

"Not a clue. G'night," I said, and hung up.

Later again, I lay in bed listening to the wireless, when the nine o'clock news came on.

One result of finding yourself momentarily in the limelight is that you want to be in it still more—and, as I was soon to discover, you can't bear it when it's switched off you altogether. I confess I was rather disappointed that the main items were about nothing more important than a threatened war between

Russia and China, a revolution in Arabia and another in the West Indies, a flood disaster in Egypt, and an American (or it may have been Russian) project to fly a cow over the moon. . . . However, right at the end, the announcer did mention what interested *me*.

"Work on the Government's new trunk road near Querbury, which should have started to-day, was held up by serious damage done to the bulldozers during last night. A Ministry of Highways spokesman has announced that the delay is temporary and that fresh equipment has already been dispatched to the site, ready to start to-morrow. Meanwhile, will anyone who may be able to give further information please get in touch with his nearest police station or with New Scotland Yard, Whitehall 1212. . . ."

I switched off both the radio and the light and, too tired and excited to sleep, lay for a while turning the whole situation over in my mind.

Not for the first time I wondered what the paper was I'd seen my father pinch off Captain Gumble's desk. Could it have been his own letter of 21st December to the D.P.C. accepting their offer? If he'd sent the letter to the Sheep's Hatch address in Querbury and then seen it—the way you *do* somehow spot your own signature in a pile of other papers —on Captain Gumble's desk at Fitchetts, might *that* be why he'd quickly pocketed it?

"Oh, dear, the grown-up world, how puzzling it is . . ." I muttered, and fell asleep.

Chapter 12

ON TUESDAY the storm broke—though nothing to what it was to be like on the next day.

Mummy had sent Friday to collect all the London dailies he could find in Brampton while she prepared breakfast. We had it in the dining-room, which gets more sun than the kitchen. He returned with an armful—and almost speechless with excitement.

" Gosh, what *did* you tell those reporters? " he said, dumping the papers on the breakfast table. "I saw Mrs. Bunn for a moment and she leered at me."

For sheer imaginative fiction, the young men we'd entertained at tea were geniuses, and to read them you'd think I had sworn to take on the Ministry of Highways single-handed, but the headings will give you an idea of the sort of stuff.

"YOU'VE GOT TO FIGHT THESE DAYS," SAYS FEBRUARY. "GOOD OLD FEB FAIRLY BASHED THOSE BULLDOZERS!" SAYS BROTHER FRIDAY. . . . THE FIGHTING CALLENDARS. . . . HER FATHER'S DAUGHTER. . . .

The photos of me, which they'd cut out of the family group at tea, looked like a St. Trinian's monster. Some of the papers gave a photo of the saucepan and all had the story of my fingerprints. (We could only suppose the detective had spilled the beans deliberately. Perhaps it was his idea of giving me a

good hiding.) One paper, which has always jeered at pro-
gressive education, even unearthed the fact that I go to a co–ed
school and implied, " what else might you expect? " But, we
noticed, they all avoided stating outright that I had *admitted*
the act—they had to be careful of libel.

Altogether enough limelight was switched on to me to
satisfy even my egotism. Only *The Times* and the *Messenger*
simply reported that the new road equipment had been
mysteriously damaged, without suggesting who might have
done it. Still, the bulldozer story was only a fleeting affair
and didn't particularly matter. What *did* matter, though it
took up only a tiny fraction of space in the Press by comparison,
was Mike Spillergun's column in the *Messenger*.

My mother, Friday and I poured over the column together
while Gail, who was less interested, settled the others to their
breakfast. She seemed a bit bung-eyed that morning and
Mummy accused her of starting a cold, but she denied it
crossly.

The column was titled "UNPACK THAT TRUNK
AND LET'S EXAMINE THE CONTENTS." It
began like this:

I must warn Sir Gilbert Notwithstanding Crump that the
fence he's sat on so restfully for the past fifteen years in his
quiet Querbury pasture is likely, in the immediate future,
to prove electric. Indeed, I'm afraid that most upright of
men will shoot right up into the air when he reads what
follows.

Recently, it will be recalled, the Minister of Highways
blew a loud blast on his trumpet and announced his plan to
beat all records with a ten-mile section of trunk road across

the downs west of Querbury, and to the south of Querbury Beacon. The section, part of the future London-Portsmouth Trunk Road, was to be finished by Easter and to cost 7½ million pounds. (What, after all, are 7½ millions to a government which—but never mind.) Nothing much was said on how the usual difficulty in such cases had been overcome; i.e. the purchase, compulsory or otherwise, of the necessary land. However, I am now able to disclose that there was in this case no difficulty at all. A firm of speculators called the Downland Preservation Company (I love that word Preservation) happened already to own a suitable stretch of downs which it had bought up since the war for a quarter of a million (my rough estimate) and which it was willing, one might suspect anxious, to sell to the Government immediately for 3½ millions. True the stretch is not the *ideal* route for the road to follow. That runs north of Querbury Beacon, across an estate owned by Lord Sprockett. Still, you can't have everything. Incidentally, Lord Sprockett although a Director of the D.P.C. is not a registered shareholder of the company, but *Messenger* readers will be relieved to hear that he is unlikely to lose by the transaction. For Sprocketts Ltd., of which he is Chairman and virtual owner, have been given the 4 million contract to build the 10-mile stretch, with an option on the rest of the road when the times comes. What the noble Lord may have lost on the take-overs he will thus gain on the fly-overs. . . .

Here a new, and somewhat equivocal, figure enters the picture in the person of Captain Horace Gumble. Captain Gumble is the Minister of Highways' brother-in-law. He is also employed by Sprocketts as their Area Manager. He is also Chairman of the Querbury District Council's Road

Committee, and the most powerful, indeed the only powerful, personality on the Council. Which may explain why the Q.U.D.C.'s consent to the new road seems to have been given quite unofficially rather than by formal resolution of the full Council as required by statute. Questioned by me on the phone about this irregularity, one Councillor replied, " Well, I was rather surprised we weren't consulted, but as it was a top priority government job I supposed they couldn't be bothered." Another Councillor similarly questioned said, " Oh, a committee can never make up its mind. After all, Captain Gumble's a very able chap—much better let him get on with it."

At this point ex-L/Cpl. M. Spillergun, R.A.O.C., who has a class-conscious prejudice about peacetime Captains, made a few inquiries at the War Office where he was, regrettably, unable to trace this particular Captain's entitlement to any military rank whatever. He did however unearth the name of a certain Pioneer Sgt. H. Gumble (doubtless no connection) who worked in 1942 on the construction of Dippenfield Aerodrome, an enterprise which, readers may recall, involved Lord Sprockett in some acrimonious publicity at the time.

But to return to the present. The new Trunk Road would appear to be quite a jolly family party, with Lord Sprockett as the family friend. Nevertheless, not a party that would provoke more than a mildly acid barb from the Spillergun, were it not for one further, and most curious, coincidence. Which is that Captain H. Gumble has a 99 per cent holding in the Downland Preservation Company.

Up till a month ago he owned merely 25 per cent of the shares, the bulk of the rest being held by a Mr. F. Bunthorpe, the Company's Managing Director. On 10th December Captain Gumble, who must by then have been well aware of the projected road, acquired the latter's holding plus a few others, completing his present total of 99 per cent. In conclusion it is worth noting that although Mr. Bunthorpe still remains the Company's registered Managing Director, the negotiations between the D.P.C. and the Ministry of Highways have throughout been conducted by Captain Gumble himself.

Well, there it is and *honi soit.* . . . Now let us change to a subject which, by contrast, exudes the scent of fresh mown lavender. . . .

The rest of the column dealt with the threatened pollution of the Thames by a new sewage works.

I don't think my brother and I quite grasped at first all the implications. But several times, as we read the page, my mother drew in her breath sharply or made tcha-tcha sounds. I assumed she was wholeheartedly with Mike Spillergun. So I was astonished when she burst out at the end: " What an utterly detestable piece. It's—oh, it's *horrible*! "

I still supposed she meant that what the D.P.C. and Captain Gumble had done was horrible. But not a bit of it. She thought it was wrong and vulgar and cruel to attack them. Women really are unpredictable. Why, only the day before she'd agreed she would fight if she knew how; and now, when someone was fighting like mad, she took the opposite side!

We went on discussing the article while we ate our own breakfast, breaking off at times to feed the others or scrape marmalade off the tablecloth.

"Does it *matter* particularly if the Gumboil does own most of the D.P.C. and is Jasper Blow's brother-in-law, and is also employed by Sprocketts?" Friday asked, tucking in to a helping of cornflakes.

"Not legally perhaps," my mother said. "But Ministers are not allowed to have a business interest in any firm which gets money from their own government department. I'm not sure whether a brother-in-law counts as a business interest, but obviously, if all this is true, Jasper Blow's in an extremely unpleasant position. I feel very sorry for him. And for Captain Gumble."

"Do you think the Government will postpone the road till there's been an inquiry?" I asked—*that* was the really important thing, I felt.

"I doubt it. I just can't imagine what the result of Mike Spillergun's article is likely to be. I'm afraid he or the *Messenger* may be sued for libel." She paused, looking thoroughly wretched. "Oh, dear, it's going to be awful whatever happens. Scandal, publicity, ill-feeling. . . . People will take sides. Life round Querbury will be poisoned. What on earth am I going to say when the Gumbles bring P. Blow to the dance?"

"Let's hope they don't bring him," said Friday cheerfully, piling butter and marmalade on to the last slice of toast. "Besides, why worry? It's nothing to do with Daddy or us what Mike Spillergun writes in his column."

"Of course it is, you half-wit. The Gumbles—*everyone*—will think Daddy's mixed up in it."

"Yes, but if Mike Spillergun is simply telling the truth . . ." Friday persisted, argumentatively. At times he wears a goofy stubborn look which infuriates her and he wore it now.

" What I don't understand is how he knew about all this at all," Gail broke in tactfully, to divert my mother and Friday from quarrelling. " Unless of course Daddy *did* tell him. . . ."

" I'm certain Daddy said nothing at all, even if he suspected something. He'll be just as horrified by the article as I am."

" Then perhaps John Gubbins told Mike Spillergun," Gail went on, trying to keep the peace, but really making matters worse. " After all, he's the Editor and he knows us awfully well. . . ."

" But as I keep telling you, knowing *us* has nothing to do with it. This has nothing to do with *us*. And yet everyone will think it has—that's what makes me so mad! "

Berry, Chrys and Des had begun to clear the remains of breakfast out to the kitchen. They are still at an age when that sort of thing is fun. We let them have their fun. Hildebrand was happy swooshing a puddle of milk and sugar around on the tray of his high chair.

I felt it was time *I* said something. The family's happiness is all my mother cares about. Now she saw it threatened, and I understood her anxiety. But nevertheless I had grown increasingly impatient with her attitude.

. " Look here, the D.P.C. and Captain Gumble played a jolly dirty trick on Daddy—trying to buy half the paddock when they knew the road was coming, so that they could make a packet. They deserve all they get. So does old Blow-his-own-trumpet, I wouldn't mind betting. What on earth does it matter *how* Mike Spillergun came to hear? Thank goodness he did. And we ought to be jolly well cheering him now, instead of moaning miserably about the possible consequences. I think his column is *marvellous*. He's a sort of champion, fighting our battle for us! "

" Oh, you're just living up to that picture of yourself in the papers," Friday jeered. " Fighting February, the one-girl Resistance Movement. . . ." Obviously my dear brother was jealous.

While he was speaking, Mummy gave me a queer look. " I think I'm beginning to have just the faintest idea how Mike Spillergun *did* come to hear something . . ." she started—when Berry ran back into the dining-room.

" There's a police car in the yard," she said. " With that man who was here yesterday. You know, the detective! He's walking round to the front door now."

" Come to arrest the bulldozer basher. That's the price of fame," said Friday. Jealousy is a terrible thing. " Shall I let him in?" he added. " Or perhaps Gail had better. She has the most welcoming smile."

But Gail was sitting in her chair as if turned to stone and with an expression of absolute terror on her face. Mummy noticed her and quickly said: " Darling, there's nothing to worry about. The tiresome little man probably just wants to apologise for having made a silly mistake yesterday. I'll let him in myself."

We heard her open the front door and say: " Oh, hallo, come in, won't you?" There was a mumbled conversation, he entered and she showed him into the living-room. Then she popped her head round the dining-room door.

" Friday, keep an eye on Hildebrand and the others for a moment. February, the detective wants a word with you."

" I want a word with him too," I said, following her to the living-room.

He stood leaning against the mantelpiece. My mother left us, closing the door.

Some general or other once said that the best means of defence is attack—or so we were taught at school. So I started off, more boldly than I felt: " Jolly decent of you to tell the papers about my fingerprints."

But he took no notice and just studied me—with a less unpleasant expression than I'd expected—stroking his chin. He still looked like a weasel, but, funnily, quite a friendly weasel this time. He also looked as if he might not have had much sleep.

Then he said calmly: " Don't let's get at cross purposes again. As a matter of fact, I had nothing to do with the papers printing that story and I'm sorry about the publicity, though —as I'll explain—it's done you a good turn. May I smoke? "

" Oh, do," I said, rather flattered to be asked.

He lit a cigarette and went on: " Of course I didn't imagine you'd done the job yourself—it was too methodical for a girl of your age, but I fancied you knew who *might* have done it."

" I've no idea," I said.

He looked at the ceiling and said casually: " Adam Henry came round to the Querbury police station an hour ago—he'd just read the papers. I'd called in from London and spoke to him myself."

" Oh, but I'm certain Adam wouldn't——"

" Then why didn't you tell me you met him at the quarry? "

" Well, I thought . . . I mean, you were already suspicious and . . ."

The detective smiled. " O.K. Let's leave it. Anyway, he told us you couldn't have done it without him knowing and I'm sure Adam is quite innocent too. But that's not why I've come now."

" Oh? Why have you come then?"

" I was passing and thought I'd drop in for a chat. I gather you've seen the papers?"

" Most of them."

" And the *Messenger*?"

" You mean Mike Spillergun's column? Yes, we were talking about it when you arrived. Have you read it?"

The detective laughed, rather grimly. " Oh, yes, I've read it. A good many hours before you did—in fact, Mike showed it to me himself last night." He stifled a yawn.

" I say," I interrupted. " Are you a Scotland Yard detective, not just a local plain-clothes man?"

" Dear me, the mask is torn off! Yes, I am actually; not that it makes all that much difference. But as I was saying, I happened to visit Mike, to talk about this and that and he showed me the column."

" He's awfully nice, isn't he?" I said. " And so funny. . . ."

" He certainly is. He likes you, too. We had quite a gossip about you."

I began to blush, unable to stop it.

" He told me I'd do much better to have you as a friend than an enemy," he continued, his eyes twinkling. " He said your head was screwed on tight and that you didn't miss much. Right?"

" Oh, I don't know . . ." I mumbled, kicking myself for feeling, and probably looking, all schoolgirlish.

" Rather an odd coincidence; I gathered from Mike that you know another friend of mine—Sir Harold Fawcett."

" Rather! Of course he's really a friend of Daddy's, but we got to know him too, about eighteen months ago. His son was our tutor. . . ."

"So Mike said. What's the son's name? I forget."

"Robin. He's an engineer and mad about canals. He wanted to open this one up again, only no one seems interested."

"Yes, I'd heard that too. I gather he's a bit of a beatnik. What's he doing nowadays?"

"Well, it's rather funny because Friday—that's my brother —saw him yesterday up at the quarry. He's working on the new road for Sprocketts—a sort of holiday job, to earn money."

The detective put his cigarette out in an ash-tray.

"Of course, this road will wreck any idea of a canal, I imagine. Did Robin tell your brother whether he minded?"

"I don't think so. Friday said he didn't seem awfully anxious to talk. He was too busy on the job."

"Ah, I expect Sprocketts keep them hard at it. By the way, I heard somewhere that Robin was also a great dog lover. Is he?" he asked casually, making to leave.

"Oh, no, dogs scare him—he told me so once. He's not exactly a dog hater, but not at all a dog lover—at least, not compared to someone like Gail. She can tame any dog by just looking at it."

"Can she? By jove! Well, thanks for the chat, February. May I take it we're now friends again?" I just grinned foolishly as I followed him into the hall.

My mother came from the kitchen and we ushered him out of the front door.

"Sorry to have troubled you, Mrs. Callendar," he said politely. And added: "You haven't had visits from the quarry this morning, I gather?"

"No, thank goodness," she said. "I suppose they've started work happily by now, though it's still surprisingly quiet."

" Not altogether surprisingly," he said, with a faint smile, and starting to walk off. " Every single bulldozer was put out of action last night again ! "

We were staggered, but I couldn't resist exclaiming: " How super ! "

" Oh, no! " Mummy said. " Not with water ? "

" Not this time. Rather more ingenious. With sand in the engine."

" But I thought they had a guard on specially? "

" They did. *And* a very fierce dog. Well, good-bye."

He walked back to the police car. We watched it drive out of the yard and up towards the quarry.

Chapter 13

"I TAKE IT YOU'RE no longer suspected," Mummy said, closing the front door.

"No." I confessed about meeting Adam at the quarry, which I hadn't mentioned before, and told her how he'd already been to the police station on my behalf.

"He's a sweet boy," she said. "I suppose they don't suspect *him*?"

"No. I'm sure they don't. By the way, that detective is from Scotland Yard. I have an idea he's investigating *more* than just the bulldozer damage."

"Nothing would surprise me less. Goodness knows what's been going on. The whole thing's crazy. When this latest news reaches London we'll have the reporters around us again like flies. You'd better lock yourself in your room—and that reminds me. Gail's gone up to bed. She's washed out. She admits she didn't sleep well last night—I'm afraid she's catching something."

By now the rest had assembled in the hall. We were discussing what to do with ourselves for the day, when Mrs. Henry telephoned, to ask if anyone would care to keep Sasha company. She said that Dr. Henry had been called out in our direction and would drop in to give whoever came a lift.

One of those family consultations followed, with my mother

holding a hand on the mouthpiece and us all shouting why we wanted, or did not want, to go and keep Sasha company. I'd already told Friday about the bulldozers, so of course he intended to rush off to the quarry. Berry, Chrys and Des all clamoured to visit Sasha, but my mother wasn't sure whether Mrs. Henry had meant to invite them. That left me. Sasha and I are both pop record fans, we share the same taste in comics and normally I'd have jumped at the chance of seeing her, but I didn't want to miss being interviewed by reporters! So I was urging Mummy to refuse the invitation when Dr. Henry himself appeared at the front door. He's a large man with a large red beard who doesn't bother with ceremony. He just barged in, booming: " Come on, February, I'm taking you back. Don't just stand there dithering. Get a move on, girl. I was supposed to be at the hospital half an hour ago for an awkward delivery. Time and childbirth wait for no man."

Somehow I never can resist Dr. Henry, so I grabbed a duffle-coat and followed him out, while Mummy continued her telephone conversation. She and Mrs. Henry gossip on the phone for hours. Probably they would still be at it by the time I got there.

" Well, Fighting February," Dr. Henry said, as we sped down the lane under branches shimmering with icicles. " I saw the papers for a moment. I don't mind you bashing Lord Sprockett's bulldozers, but you're overdoing it when you start bashing his Irish workmen as well—remember I'm an Irishman myself. I've just come from the quarry."

" Why? What's the matter? "

" They left a guard on last night. A big Irishman called Paddy and another chap—a cockney, I think. Also a savage dog. When the rest of them arrived to work in the dark this morning, the dog was there O.K. But no sign of the other two. Then the workmen tried to start up the machines and found they'd been damaged again. Then, with daylight, they discovered Paddy lying semi-conscious in a bush."

" Gosh! What had happened to him? "

" A nasty bang on the head with a blunt instrument. He'd been drinking too. Probably a quarrel. He's all right—I've sent him off to hospital in an ambulance. He can't remember anything yet—not even if he did have a quarrel."

" Where's the other one—the cockney? "

" Lord knows—the police are after him. Captain Gumble himself is there now—blowing off his top. I didn't ask him if he'd· read the *Messenger* this morning! " Dr. Henry turned towards me, gave a broad grin and winked.

" You know, that *Messenger* article had nothing to do with Daddy," I explained.

" Oh, sure, sure," he said, obviously not believing me. I began to understand what my mother had meant. Then he added, with a chuckle: "By the way, I suppose you *didn't* have anything to do with that bulldozer nonsense? Either night? "

" Nothing at all." I told him how Adam had already been to the police. As I'd guessed, Adam had not mentioned that to his parents! Dr. Henry drove in silence for a while, puffing at his pipe. We came in sight of the little bridge over the Quer.

" Adam's a funny chap," he said. " I noticed him slip away on his bike before finishing breakfast and supposed he had an early start at the rep. Typical of him to say nothing—he wouldn't even tell us if he got himself hung for murder. Probably you know him better than I do. Do you think he'll make anything of this acting? "

" Oh, yes, I think he's going to be a marvellous actor!"

" Hmm . . ."

As we crested the bridge we saw the seven swans on the water nearby and Dr. Henry slowed down to study them. The two parents rested by the bank and the five young ones seemed to be sailing off independently upstream.

" Ah, me, parents and children." He spoke rather sadly. " We love each other underneath, I dare say, but we go our own ways all the same. *Don't* we, February?"

" I suppose we do, rather," I said.

" Which reminds me, I ran into your friend Robin Fawcett working for Sprocketts up at the quarry just now—another young man who's a worry to his father, unless I'm mistaken."

" I don't think he is any more. I haven't seen him for ages, but Friday met him at the quarry on Sunday."

" Quite a gang of them with him—mostly students. They didn't appear to be taking the damage too seriously—in fact, one of them was strumming on a guitar as there was nothing else to do."

" Did you chat to Robin?"

" Not properly. I was too busy patching up the Irishman. Besides, there's never much to say to beatniks. Isn't that the word at present? I like them all right. In fact, I like most young people, especially when they have beards. But I rather wish they'd wash."

" What's the point of washing if you're working in icy conditions on a new road?"

" Perhaps you're right. I'm getting stuffy and middle-aged. I admit I was just as unwashed myself in my younger days; and just as bolshie. *And* I couldn't even play the guitar."

He stopped the car at Brampton, to buy tobacco at the

stores, and I went in with him to buy a few sweets for Sasha. This time Mrs. Bunn herself was there, gossiping with a crowd of customers. They all ceased talking when we entered and it wasn't hard to guess their topic.

One of the assistants served Dr. Henry. Mrs. Bunn, with a side glance at the customers, addressed me. " Hallo, dear. Been reading about you. Quite the celebrity."

" Oh, that. A packet of mixed boiled, please."

" Have it on the house, dear, seeing as how you've been so *busy* lately," she said, handing me the paper bag. " I enjoyed reading your Dad in the *Messenger* this morning too." She gave another side glance at the audience, who tittered.

" Daddy didn't write anything. That was Mike Spillergun," I mumbled, embarrassed and angry.

" All comes to the same, dear, doesn't it?"

The buzz of conversation began again as we left.

In the car, Dr. Henry relit his pipe before driving on. " A nasty piece of work, that woman—though I shouldn't say so of one of my patients."

Dr. Henry has had a practice in Querbury for fifteen years and knows the place and everyone to do with it inside out. Usually he's as discreet as a tomb, but he seemed chatty this morning so I asked what he thought of Mr. Bunn.

" Oh, Fred Bunn's not a bad chap. Just lazy and rather vain. A bit of a fool really. His wife runs him behind the scenes."

" He must be a pretty good farmer—I mean, he farms an awful lot of land round here."

" Useless, I'm told. Can't think how he gets by, except that he's said to have various other irons in the fire. He's a Londoner really; so is she. They settled here during the war to escape the blitz and started farming. They were in partnership with

Gumble when I first came, but I forget what at. Gumble wasn't much in those days, but he seems to have done all right for himself since then. Marrying Jasper Blow's sister may have helped. . . ."

"Do you know anyone in Querbury called Bunthorpe?"

"Bunthorpe? No, I've never heard of the name in Querbury, though it *is* vaguely familiar from somewhere."

I didn't remind him of the *Messenger* article. Besides, we had reached his gate. He dropped me and drove on. I ran down the short drive to the house, where I found Sasha playing through her pop favourites. To look at, Sasha's a gorgeous creature, with long fair hair, great blue eyes and a row of teeth when she smiles like a toothpaste ad. She could easily be a model or a beauty queen or a film star or something of that sort when she grows up, except that she happens also to have a brain. She's at the Querbury Grammar School and will almost certainly get a scholarship to the university some day. In short, she has everything I haven't and I ought to be wildly envious, but as a matter of fact, I'm not—probably because, on top of everything else, she's so jolly *nice*.

We played pop records most of the morning. There is nothing like Cliff Richard, Adam Faith, Dave Sampson and the rest to take your mind off your worries and I quite forgot the road and everything to do with it until half an hour before lunch. We'd strolled out into the garden to work up an appetite and I suddenly found myself explaining the whole situation to her.

" Let me get it straight," she said when I'd finished. " You told John Gubbins what you'd found out, and he obviously put Mike Spillergun on the job to find out more. Then last Saturday Mike Spillergun came down to see you himself and said he intended to make such a rumpus in his column that the Government might stop the road and hold an inquiry. Right, so far? "

" Yes. The funny thing is that when I said I was afraid they'd start work on Monday—that's yesterday—in any case, he said: " You never can tell." Thinking back on it, I can't help wondering if he *knew* the bulldozers would be damaged on Sunday night. Last night, too, possibly."

Sasha prodded a rhododendron bush with a twig, knocking a little shower of icicles to the ground.

" The bulldozer business has certainly helped to focus public attention on the road," she said thoughtfully. " All the papers are bound to take Mike Spillergun's story up now, I imagine. Of course it may be just a lucky coincidence; someone local may have done it. But if we assume Mike Spillergun *did* know —had perhaps even *planned* the damage as part of his campaign —then that almost certainly rules local people out."

" Another puzzling thing is the bit he mentioned about Captain Gumble buying up all the shares in the D.P.C. Do you understand about shares? "

" Not particularly, but we had a lecture on it at school last term. It's like this, more or less. Supposing you buy a hundred shares in a company at a moment when each share costs one pound and the company does badly so that the value of the shares falls to ten shillings. Then you've lost fifty pounds, if you want to sell out. Alternately, if the company does well and the shares rise in value, you'll make."

" I see. So if you happen to have private information that the company is about to do very well indeed, do you quickly buy all the shares you can? "

" You jolly well do, I should think."

" But the people you've bought them from are pretty sick afterwards, aren't they? "

" I bet they are."

" Then I should think Mr. Bunthorpe, whoever he is, must be awfully fed up with Captain Gumble at this minute, because apparently Captain Gumble bought all his shares in the D.P.C. a few months ago and I should imagine that, with this road, the shares are several times more valuable."

" Bound to be. Who is Mr. Bunthorpe? "

"Well, he's the Managing Director apparently of the D.P.C. I saw a letter of Daddy's addressed to the D.P.C. in

Querbury, so I suppose he's there. But when I asked your father if he knew him—he didn't. And that's odd, because your father knows *everyone*."

" What was the address in Querbury? Do you remember?"

" Yes. 3 Sheep's Hatch. The funny name stuck in my mind."

Mrs. Henry came out, shouting: " Lunch ready, girls. Where are you?"

" Coming," we shouted back, and walked towards the house.

" I tell you what," Sasha said suddenly. " My mother's got to go shopping in Querbury this afternoon. Let's go with her and try to find out who Mr. Bunthorpe is."

Dr. Henry's surgery is in a side street, on a bend in the road. The Odeon Cinema is just past the bend, with the police station next to it. The surgery has its own little car park in front and Mrs. Henry parked her car there, behind Dr. Henry's. We slipped in by a side door, avoiding the waiting-room, to see him for a moment before the afternoon consultations began. We found him busy filling hypodermic syringes, sharpening scalpels, testing chloroform masks and mixing poisonous concoctions, like every other G.P. preparing to face his patients at 2 p.m. In other words he was lying on a couch, smoking a pipe and reading a detective story.

" Won't keep you a moment," Mrs. Henry said. " Just wanted to borrow some money to save me going to the bank. There's a record crowd in the waiting-room by the look of it."

" Let them wait," Dr. Henry said cheerfully. " They've got something to talk about for once."

" How do you mean?" Sasha asked.

He told us that sleepy old Querbury was buzzing with what had been in the morning papers and that now the latest news from the quarry had worked the town up to a fever of excitement. Nothing spectacular had occurred in Querbury since Mafeking Night in 1900 (when someone set the Town Hall on fire). Like its M.P., Sir Gilbert Crump, it was fairly shooting up into the air with the present scandal.

"Everyone's convinced that 'Mike Spillergun' is merely your father's nom-de-plume and that you or Friday fixed the machines *both* nights," Dr. Henry said, chuckling. "I've assured them they're quite wrong, but of course they still remain convinced. They prefer it that way."

"Are they against us mostly?" I asked.

"Against you! Good lord, you're a blooming hero! No one cares much for either Sprockett or Gumble. They think this is the funniest thing that ever happened. I'm not sure it won't start a revolution. You'd better do your shopping secretly, if you don't want people pestering you for your autograph or an exclusive interview. The place is lousy with reporters—I even had one of them in here."

"What did you tell him?" Mrs. Henry asked rather anxiously—her husband is liable to get violent with people who waste his time.

"Oh, I just pretended to think he'd come as a patient. I shoved him protesting on to this couch, and grabbed an oxygen mask and a large knife and told him not to worry, he wouldn't feel anything, and that it was much better to have it out at once rather than wait for a hospital bed. . . . I'm afraid he left rather hurriedly in the end."

Mrs. Henry sighed. "One of these days you'll end up hurriedly—in front of the General Medical Council. By the way, the girls are meeting me here about half past three. They seem to think they can amuse themselves till then. I'm running February home for tea."

"I'll see the door's left open for you. I'm going up to the hospital after surgery. The Irishman's feeling better and I want a chat with him. I know you have an insatiable love for publicity," Dr. Henry added to me as we went. " But all the same, I'd keep your head covered with your duffle hood and behave a bit stealthily if you're shopping. There really are quite a lot of people around Querbury this afternoon who'd like a word with you, I suspect."

"Don't worry," I said, pulling the hood on against the cold. "Sasha and I intended to behave stealthily in any case."

Chapter 14

WE'D LOOKED up Sheep's Hatch in a Town Directory in her house before leaving. It was a little alley, which I'd passed scores of times without noticing its name, off an old street called Market Road, a cul-de-sac. Market Road opens off the High Street, bends round and runs parallel to it for a hundred yards and then finishes at the Gas Works which must have been built on the site of the original market. Except for Southern Gas Board coal lorries which frequently get jammed there, the street has little traffic. The houses are chiefly used by professional people like estate agents, solicitors and dentists or small businesses like tailors, shoemakers and furniture menders, who don't mind being away from the crowds—in fact, prefer to be.

Querbury has a great many old houses with overhanging first stories and comic beams set all ways into the front. They were mostly built to look like that about fifty years ago. But the Market Road houses are genuinely old—indeed the street is what's called a show piece. It even has cobbles. When Sasha and I entered it from the busy High Street, the roar of buses, lorries and motor bikes seemed far away suddenly. The sky threatened snow and there was hardly anyone in sight which increased our sense of adventure and though we really kept on the duffle-coat hoods against the cold, they added to a pleasantly conspiratorial feeling.

Sheep's Hatch was some distance beyond the bend in Market Road, a dark alley about twenty yards long, also paved with cobbles, and finishing in a little courtyard. There were several deeply recessed doorways on either side, as well as two or three in the end courtyard belonging to houses which looked too derelict to be occupied, except for the fact that outside they had dust-bins, an ancient pram and a single pair of patched pyjamas on a tattered washing-line.

We stood a moment at the alley's mouth, slightly funking going in. Then we walked a few paces farther, to look at an antique shop. The window was crammed with junk of every description; blue and white china, old books, brass candle-sticks, a rag doll, three yellow bottle-shaped gourds with wooden stoppers. . . . A lorry, bringing coal from the station, rattled past and drove on through the Gas Works gates at the end of Market Road. Silence surrounded us again.

"I don't see what we do exactly when we find Number Three Sheep's Hatch," I said doubtfully.

"Let's find it first," said Sasha.

As she spoke, several footsteps clattered down a staircase close at hand inside the alley. A door opened and a familiar voice said heartily: "Splendid. Well, enjoy yourselves at the flick. My car's in the Odeon car park and I'll meet you there at half past four."

Then, without shutting the door, Captain Gumble ascended the stairs. Other footsteps came slowly down the alley towards us.

"I'm so glad you'll be at their ghastly dance next week," drawled an affected girl's voice—I knew it well.

" Doubt if I shall be allowed to go now," came the reply, and I recognised that voice too.

" The father's a complete crook of course, so *my* father always says. And February reeks of man-ewer. But the rest aren't too bad in their provin-shull way."

" Oh, February's all right—just uncivilised," said P. Blow. " Actually, I think they're a particularly nice family, but we won't argue about it. However, you'll have gathered that as far as my uncle's concerned, they're out."

" I just *adore* your uncle, Peter. Too sweet."

" Oh, do you? Between ourselves he's an absolute stinker, but I'm fond of my aunt. Well, we'd better hurry if you insist on seeing that film."

Before they emerged from Sheep's Hatch I had grabbed Sasha and dragged her with me into the antique shop. Peeping out through the glass I watched them walk up Market Road towards the High Street. Helen Ponton was wearing ridiculous stiletto heels which kept turning over on the cobbles. P. Blow, as far as I could judge from his back view, looked jolly bored with her, I thought.

" And what can I do for you ladies?" said the shop's owner, an untidy bespectacled old man with a smarmy voice.

" How much are those three gourds?" I asked, pointing to the window.

" Fifty-two shillings."

" They're not worth more than sixpence," I said haughtily. Before he'd recovered, I had dragged Sasha outside again and round the corner into Sheep's Hatch.

" I say, wasn't that Captain Gumble's nephew with what's-her-name, that girl the Sprocketts adopted?" Sasha whispered.

" Yup. Sssh!"

We were half-way along the alley, outside what I took to be the door Captain Gumble had left unshut. It had a brass 3 on it, but no signs of an office name-plate. The door opened on to a short steep flight of stairs, at the top of which another door stood slightly ajar. In the room beyond several voices were talking angrily at once. An argument appeared to be brewing.

"I'm sorry you didn't like them coming here," I heard Captain Gumble say irritably. "But I can't imagine what harm it could do. Besides, I had to meet them somewhere, to fix a rendezvous for after their flick and this was the easiest place."

A woman spoke—she sounded extraordinarily like Mrs. Bunn. "Oh, I don't worry about her—she's a daft creature, anyway. But that nephew of yours is different. Sharp as a pin—I didn't like the way he kept peering at the papers and things round the office."

"My good woman, he wasn't here more than five minutes and he wouldn't have been that long if Fred hadn't gossiped about horses."

Mrs. Bunn, for it certainly was her, sounded nearly hysterical with rage. "Don't you 'my good woman' me, Horace Gumble! *Captain* Horace Gumble. Pah! You were glad enough to call me Elsie not so many years back and don't you forget it."

"If you must know, I couldn't care less what I call you," said Captain Gumble, evidently no less angry, but under better control. "This happens to be one of my offices and I really must ask you to say whatever it is you want to say quickly."

By now Sasha and I were too enthralled to think of caution

and stepped right inside the doorway in our eagerness to catch everything they said.

" *Your* office. I like that. Who's Managing Director of the D.P.C.? Who took the risk signing himself ' Bunthorpe ' all these years? "

" Exactly. Who *did* sign himself Bunthorpe? Not me. Signing a false name on legal documents happens to be rather a serious offence." Captain Gumble spoke more calmly, but there was something in his tone which made even me shiver, though I hardly understood what he meant. Mrs. Bunn understood well enough, I guessed. She didn't answer for a moment; then said venomously: " Fred, don't just stand there like a sick cow, gulping and letting him get away with it! *Say* something, man! "

" Well, Fred? Do I gather you and your wife feel you have some grievance? " The voice cracked like a whip. Poor Mr. Bunn. I could just imagine him gulping and going red in the face, struggling for the words.

" It's like this, Horace, Elsie and I reckon we've got a grievance all right, your buying us out, when you knew about this road coming."

" Ah. So that's it. You've been reading the papers. God knows who gave Spillergun that story. I'm pretty sure it wasn't Callendar—as far as I'm aware, he hadn't the smallest suspicion I was connected with the D.P.C. No one had, till this morning. I'll wring that chap Spillergun's neck if I ever meet him."

" Well, you got me to write that letter to Callendar about buying his field so I thought maybe you'd said something to him too—on the side. ...."

" Not a word—never met the chap except for a moment

when he came to a party a week or two ago. Actually, I forget if I told you, he wrote afterwards cancelling the sale and returning our cheque. I've been meaning to check up on the legal position about that, but the maddening thing is I can't now find his first letter accepting our offer. I remember taking the file home from here one night and I'm certain I had it then."

Mrs. Bunn snorted contemptuously. "Callendar's another slimy one, no mistake. All high ideals on top, crooked as they come under it. Of course he wrote that stuff himself in the *Messenger*, or put Spillergun up to it. Best job he ever did too, if it fixes your hash." She snorted again.

"My dear Elsie," Captain Gumble replied blandly. "My hash is my business. Let's stick to yours. I bought both of you out of the company at a very fair price. You've doubled your capital. Now you're complaining because you think you might have made still more by staying in. Is that right?"

"Course we'd have made more—a great deal more, same as you have," said Mr. Bunn, aggressive now. "You out-smarted us, Horace, and we're not standing for it, see?"

"Then, do I understand that you'd like to buy the lot back?" Captain Gumble's voice had changed to an almost genial note; all the more suspicious, at least so I thought.

"Well . . ." Mr. Bunn didn't sound certain that he would like to buy his lot back.

"Come on. Make your mind up. Rather than have you and Elsie nursing a grievance I'm prepared to sell you *my whole present stock* in the company at the price I gave you for yours. That is, about £226,000 altogether. Call it £225,000 between old friends. As you've read in this morning's *Messenger* the Government are likely to buy the land for three millions.

I'm offering you the chance of a fortune. I'm sick to death of the D.P.C. It's been nothing but a trouble from the start. You can have it—for £225,000. And when you've cleared two and three-quarter millions I hope you'll show a little more gratitude."

" Bet there's a snag in it somewhere," I couldn't resist murmuring to Sasha, who grinned. Mrs. Bunn's next remark showed that she saw what the snag could be.

" The Government haven't paid up yet, then?"

" Not yet. There are various formalities. But they will, when the stretch of road is finished. Here's the Ministry of Highways' file. You can check it through in half a minute for yourself to see I'm on the level."

" Wait a moment. *Wait a moment.*" Mrs. Bunn's voice rose again in anger. " How do we know the road *will* be finished? It hasn't started yet!"

" Oh, that nonsense. A temporary hold-up—hooligans. The police are on to them. The Minister, my brother-in-law, assured me himself this morning on the phone that he intends to have it ready on schedule whatever happens. We, Sprocketts, are going right ahead to-morrow."

There was an awed hush upstairs. Then Captain Gumble spoke again. " I've made the offer and I shan't repeat it. Barclay's Bank shuts in twenty minutes. If you want to accept, we'll go round together now. If you don't, please leave me in peace. I'm a very busy man."

Mr. and Mrs. Bunn could be heard consulting. There was a rustle of paper, as if they were quickly reading through the correspondence. It seemed obvious, even to me, that Captain Gumble wouldn't present them with two and three-quarter millions unless he had to for some reason. Could it be that

Mike Spillergun's article had frightened him off; or perhaps that he knew the road was *not* going ahead after all? But greed's a blinding force. The Bunns, it seemed, had decided to accept the offer. We heard her say they'd go with him to the bank, and pay the cheque over there.

"Splendid! Now you're showing some sense," Captain Gumble said in his familiar hearty way.

"Golly, you're a twister if ever there was one," I muttered. And nearly had a fit when a voice immediately behind whispered: "Sssh, child."

Chapter 15

WE SWUNG ROUND. Mike Spillergun stood framed in the door and with his finger to his lips. Footsteps were heard on the floor of the room above. He beckoned and we tiptoed after him like lightning out of the alley. In Market Road he grabbed each of us by an arm and, almost carrying us, strode at a fantastic speed towards the High Street.

" A father and his daughters out for a brisk walk in the cold—at least, that's what I *hope* they think if they see us from behind." He laughed. " I have the strongest objection to Captain Gumble wringing my neck."

" By the way, this is my friend Sasha Henry," I said, short of breath, as we rounded the bend in Market Road. " Sasha, this is Mike Spillergun."

" Hiya, Sasha. No time now for a polite interchange about the weather or other equally absorbing topics. Isn't there a little café where this road joins the main street? I remember seeing one as I passed."

" The Stuffed Owl probably," I said.

" Let's have a quick chat in there, so we can examine the cards in our hand."

" Oh, *rather*," Sasha and I agreed.

The Stuffed Owl Tea Shoppe is one of the old half-timbered

Querbury houses built fifty years ago. You go down steps to enter and have a good private view of passers-by in the street above. A minute later the three of us were at a corner table, half-hidden by one of the olde worlde wooden columns which pretend to hold up the ceiling. And a minute after that we saw Mr. and Mrs. Bunn hurry by—in the direction of Barclay's Bank.

" There goes the mysterious F. Bunthorpe," Mike Spillergun said, with a smile. " I'll give you three guesses what Mrs. Bunn's maiden name was."

" Thorpe," Sasha said immediately—that girl really has a brain.

They were followed at a few paces by Captain Gumble who evidently did not wish to be seen too obviously with them. He was whistling and appeared pleased with himself.

" For a man who is about to sacrifice the chance of making two and three-quarter millions, the gallant captain looks extraordinarily cheerful, don't you think?" said Mike Spillergun.

We held off discussing things properly till the waitress took our order. She was the modern sort of waitress, with her hair piled high like a beehive, a short skirt, long dirty finger-nails varnished mauve, and a sulky expression as if taking the order was an enormous sacrifice of her dignity, but not one she intended to make much longer if she could help it.

Sasha and I had eaten a large meal with Mrs. Henry, so we asked merely for two cups of tea.

" Three teas then?" the waitress snapped, making off impatiently.

" No, just a moment," Mike said, studying the menu. " I've had no lunch, no breakfast and very little dinner last night, so I shall have scrambled eggs, mushrooms, bacon and buttered toast."

" Mushrooms are off. Anyway, we don't do lunch after two-thirty."

" Well, then, double the buttered toast."

" We don't do buttered toast before three-thirty."

" Well, then, a large cup of coffee."

" Black or white ? "

" White, please."

" The milk's run out. The manageress has sent for some more. We've only got enough for teas." She yawned, raised one lot of mauve nails to her mouth, breathed on them and then polished them on the back of the order pad. Mike studied her for a moment and said pleasantly: " You have a face like a doughnut and a mind like the vestigial dollop of jam inside."

She didn't flicker an eyelid. " Don't do doughnuts. Just three teas then." And she tittuped off, not even bothering to wait for a reply.

" I suppose both of you will be like that in another year or two," he sighed. " But one mustn't complain. It's nice and restful in here at least. Let's get down to business. What were you doing eavesdropping ? "

" We were trying to find out who Mr. Bunthorpe was— and did find out ! "

" Great minds think alike—I had a similar idea myself."

" Were you there behind us all the time ? "

" Most of it. I'd just entered the street when you nipped out of that shop and into the alley. I nipped after you."

" Then you must have passed P. Blow and Helen Ponton." I told him who they were.

" Um. I should think Gumble's pretty keen to have his nephew taking out Sprockett's adopted daughter."

" Well, P. Blow seemed pretty keen on Helen himself the last time I saw them."

" I fancy he's changed his mind by now. I've never seen a young man look more bored and exasperated by a girl in my life! "

" How did you get here? "

" Your father drove me and John Gubbins down. They dropped me in Querbury before going on to see your M.P., Sir Gilbert Crump. Proper flap behind the scenes. I believe Jasper Blow himself is here too, with Crump, to try to sort things out. Every paper in the country will be attacking him to-morrow and he's got to be able to make some kind of statement! Even Scotland Yard's interested. . . ."

" Oh, yes. A detective who knows you came yesterday and again this morning."

" He told me." Mike Spillergun grinned. " By the way, I hope you didn't mind all that publicity I gave you."

" So it was *you* who tipped off the papers! "

" Yes, I'm afraid I spillergunned the beans! Nothing like starting a few red herrings when you've got a really hot story. To-morrow the other papers will still be rehashing what I said to-day. I shall already have moved on. The column is usually Tuesday and Thursday, but John Gubbins wants me to do one to-morrow as well."

" What are you going to say? " Sasha asked.

" Not sure yet. But it's good to have a few trumps up your sleeve. What we heard together in Sheep's Hatch will do very nicely for one trump, don't you think? "

The waitress brought the cups and banged them down, slopping the tea into the saucers.

" Tell me, dear, do you find bees keep hiving in your hair-do? " Mike asked. But she didn't seem to follow.

" The manageress says she can manage some baked beans if you're hungry," she said, sneering.

" On toast? "

" Don't do toast before three-thirty."

" Please thank the manageress most cordially, and ask if I could have just one bean lightly baked in butter."

" We don't do one bean. Just the tin or nothing."

" Right. Just the tin—but without the label."

" I'll have to ask the manageress," she said, tittuping off again.

We speculated whether she was a nitwit or just a wit. " Often there's not so much difference," said Mike.

Remembering my conversation with Sasha before lunch, I asked: " I say, when you told me last Saturday that maybe work wouldn't start on Monday, did you *know* someone was going to bash the bulldozers? "

Mike looked mockingly at me. " My dear girl, what intelligent questions you do ask."

" It was Sasha's idea really. She thought all that publicity certainly helped focus attention on your column."

" You did, did you, Sasha? Then you're a bright girl. You should have no trouble with your 'A' level."

" But *did* you know? " she asked eagerly.

He leant across the table and placed a finger on his nose. " I'll let you both into a secret. I *thought* I knew. But now I suspect I was wrong."

This was too tantalising. But it spurred my brain to a

flash of inspiration. "Surely you don't mean Robin and the other beatniks? You said you'd met them a few days before, I remember."

But Mike simply smiled mischievously.

While I sipped my tea, thoughts fizzed through my head in all directions. Suddenly the idea seemed obvious. Why hadn't it even occurred to me? Just the sort of crazy gesture Robin would make to save the canal. And he could easily have slipped back to the quarry on Sunday—he knew the whole area like the palm of his hand. But what about last night, when Paddy and the cockney had been on guard? I knew Robin would never hit someone with a blunt instrument— he was an ardent pacifist.

"Come on, you *must* tell us, *please*," Sasha and I pleaded. But we could see he had no intention of doing so.

"Sorry, not yet. That's one of the trumps I'm keeping up my sleeve. By the way, don't forget I'm coming to your dance to-morrow, if I can make it."

"Really, the dance! We can't possibly have it now."

"Of course you must. You can't cancel important things like a dance because of a national scandal at your back door! Remember Drake's bowls. Remember Nero fiddling. . . ."

"But your dance isn't *to-morrow*!" Sasha exclaimed. "I'm almost sure the invitation said a date next week. I haven't even thought yet what I'm going to wear!"

The waitress was with us again. "The manageress says she's sorry, but she can't cook you the tin without the label."

Mike gave a loud guffaw. "Thank God, I really do believe you're just a wit after all." But her doughnut face never changed expression and I'm still not certain in my mind that he was right.

The Stuffed Owl was filling up with customers having an early tea. At the next table two Querbury women discussed the news confidentially in voices that would have penetrated the hull of an aircraft-carrier.

" Rachel said there's a meeting going on this minute in the Council Offices."

" Of course the whole lot of them are in it up to the eyes. They'll have to resign, I should think, and have a fresh election."

" Rachel said Sir Gilbert Crump's involved too. Jasper Blow himself is there with him now and a crowd of others in the Agent's office. She saw them through the window."

" I should have thought Crump was above that sort of thing."

" Don't you believe it. Rachel said she heard that Gumble promised him a rake-off from the start. . . ."

Mike Spillergun left money for the bill and we all went outside. It had started to snow.

" At least Querbury's enjoying itself," he said in the street. " I'm a public benefactor if nothing else. Well, thanks for our talk. Which is the way to the hospital? I want a chat with that Irishman."

We showed him. " Thanks awfully for the tea," Sasha said. " We're supposed to be meeting my mother now."

" Good-bye. And good-bye, February. We may possibly meet later to-day. I'm not sure of my plans yet."

" Excuse me, Mr. Spillergun," said a voice at our elbow. The spectacled journalist who looked like a blond tortoise was standing beside us. " Could I just ask you some questions? "

"You could *not*. But if you're after a really inside story I can tell you where you'll find one." Mike took him by the arm and pointed through the window to the two Querbury women seated at their table. "Go and chat to them. They know *everything*."

"Thanks awfully, Mr. Spillergun. I certainly will."

Chapter 16

WE SEPARATED from Mike and spent about ten minutes browsing round Woolworths. When we came out the sky was pitch dark though the hour was still only three-fifteen. The snow was falling as if it really meant business, a relentless deluge of flakes lit up by the shops and street lamps. A layer of icing covered the pavement an inch deep and as Sasha and I wore thin shoes we decided to bolt for the surgery.

Our feet were nearly frozen when we reached there. We darted first into a paper shop opposite, to stock up with comics in case we had to wait long for Mrs. Henry. No one can complain that the selection of comics is limited nowadays. It took us ten minutes to make our choice. By the time we emerged a further inch or two of snow covered the ground. The street was almost deserted. We stood in the doorway, tucking the comics into our coats, when a large black Jaguar saloon turned out of the Odeon car park and roared past us, sending up a spray of snow. We caught merely a fleeting glimpse of the driver, a large man in a checked cap, his moustaches protruding beyond the upturned collar of an ulster.

We watched the car skid slightly as it slowed down at the junction with the High Street. Then it turned left in the direction of Chichester and Portsmouth.

"That looked rather like Captain Gumble," Sasha said. "He seemed in a hurry."

"It certainly was Captain Gumble. There was no one else with him. I suppose he's coming back to collect P. Blow and Helen Ponton later."

Sasha found she had left a comic on the counter and went in again to fetch it, while I waited for her, wondering about Captain Gumble. She returned and we crossed to the surgery. The side door had been left unlocked and as we were about to enter, another car rounded the corner gathering speed, then pulled up abruptly near us. It also was a dark saloon, but with the word POLICE illuminated on top. A head was thrust out of the left-hand window and a voice I recognised as the detective's shouted: "Did you girls happen to see a black Jaguar go by a minute ago?"

"Yes, if you mean Captain Gumble," I said. "He's only just gone by."

"Oh, hallo, it's February Callendar. You didn't notice which way he turned in the High Street?"

"Left—towards Chichester. He was in a hurry. So will you have to be, if you're trying to catch up with him!"

"Thanks, February. I'll buy you an ice-cream some day." The Scotland Yard detective withdrew his head, spoke to the police driver beside him and the car fairly shot off.

"Wouldn't I just *love* to know what that's all about!"

"Do you think . . ." Sasha began, but I cut her short.

"Let's get inside. My brain's frozen."

There was a gas-fire in Dr. Henry's room, and we warmed ourselves by that for a while, pondering the afternoon's many strange events. The comics had lost their appeal. Real life seemed more interesting.

"I suppose this is silly," she said thoughtfully. "But do you think that possibly Captain Gumble was doing a bunk? I mean, out of the country? Southampton's only an hour's drive. Or Gosport."

"That's rather far fetched. I should think he was simply driving home in a hurry. Besides, why should he do a bunk?"

"Well, I've been wondering. It seems awfully unlikely that he'd give up all chance of making the three millions himself, unless he had some reason for wanting £225,000 *at once*. He could have been bluffing when he told the Bunns that the road was going ahead. Perhaps he knows the whole deal is off and he's taking what he can quickly."

"Yes, but why do a bunk?"

"Well, even if the Bunns did forge the name Bunthorpe, Gumble himself is pretty well implicated, I should think. There's something fishy about the whole D.P.C. set-up. Perhaps that's why that Scotland Yard man came down— and why he's chasing after him now—to catch him before he can slip abroad."

"What *I* wonder is who bashed the bulldozers. And why. That's connected with it all somewhere too, I'm certain."

The surgery door burst open and in staggered the most miserable object I've ever seen: Helen Ponton. Her smart fur hat and coat were bedraggled with damp snow, with fresh snow on top; her shoes also were soaked and the stiletto heel had come off one of them; her face was blue; her teeth were chattering; her eyes were red and swollen with tears; her nose was running and she made a whimpering noise like a sick dog.

To our further astonishment Adam came in with her, half-holding her up with one arm. He closed the door with the other.

"What on earth . . ." Sasha and I exclaimed.

"I found her hobbling up the street outside the theatre. I'd nipped out to buy some cigarettes for the producer. As far as I can make out, she was trying to walk all the way to Deans, so I thought the best thing was to bring her to the surgery and ring up the Sprocketts. I didn't expect to find you here."

I seemed to spend my life either being sorry for Helen or else hating her. Now I felt sorry for her. With Sasha's help I stripped off her clothes, wrapped her in a blanket and thawed her out on a chair in front of the fire, while Adam brewed up some cocoa. Dr. Henry always keeps cocoa in the surgery for shock. We've enjoyed the shock many a time.

Adam was obviously eager to get back to the rep. "We've another rehearsal at four and the producer will be wondering where I've gone."

"We'll cope. Mummy will be here any minute."

"I say, thanks awfully for telling the police . . ." I began, but he mumbled about it being nothing and disappeared again into the blizzard. I'm just sure that boy will go far some day —if not as an actor, then as something else.

I'd found a bottle of medicinal brandy and put a large shot in Helen's cocoa. Forcing it between her chattering teeth, the way I've seen it done on the telly, I said: "Here, drink this, luv."

The gas-fire, or it may have been the cocoa, bucked her up no end. She stopped the whimpering noise and began to answer our questions quite sensibly. She told us (of course she had no idea we already knew) that she and P. Blow had been to the cinema. But the film was rotten and he had insisted on leaving after an hour.

"We found it was snowing so I wanted to go back in and watch till four-thirty, because his uncle was meeting us then. Peter wanted to stroll round the shops instead, but I just couldn't walk through the snow in these shoes, could I?" she said plaintively.

We made sympathetic sounds, and I asked: "You know Peter Blow quite well, do you?"

"Oh, yes, *awfully* well. At least, I thought so. I'm not sure now. We met at a party about a fortnight ago—oh, yes, you were both there, too, of course—and then Mrs. Gumble asked me over one day after he'd had a fall hunting and was laid up in bed."

"You mean he fell off?" Sasha asked in all innocence.

"Oh, no, he's a *frightfully* good horseman. Some clumsy fool who couldn't ride properly jumped on to him."

"Is that what he told you?" I asked sharply.

"Yes, at least I *think* so. Anyway, he was fed up being in bed and we played halma and discussed books and things. He's *frightfully* clever and amusing, you know."

"He certainly has a terrific sense of humour," I said.

"Yes, hasn't he? Well, it was great fun, so I went over there several times and he came to us because his father is a friend of my father's."

By now I was not feeling quite so sorry for her any more, so I asked impatiently: "As your charming relationship progressed did he ever mention the new trunk road?"

"Oh, but we *often* discussed it. That's how the trouble all started, really. And this afternoon at the cinema. I mean that's why he and his uncle quarrelled. . . ." She became confused and tearful again.

"Don't keep on butting in. Let her tell the story *her* way," Sasha said.

So I nobly restrained my curiosity and gave her another dollop of brandy in her cocoa and this was what the story amounted to, including some of what I could read between the lines for myself.

Pretty obviously Captain Gumble had encouraged the friendship between his nephew and Lord Sprockett's adopted daughter for all he was worth. Peter Blow had been fairly keen too, at first, because old Helen's not too bad to look at of her type. Anyway, she had travelled and wore smart clothes and was obviously stuck on him, so that until he could start riding again it was probably slightly more fun seeing her than seeing no one, I imagine.

But the budding friendship came its first cropper on the subject of the road. Helen was all for the road, because of Lord Sprockett. She imagined P. Blow would be too, on account of his uncle, not to mention his father.

"Captain and Mrs. Gumble brought him over with them to lunch the day all the papers announced it," she told us. "That M.P.—what's his name?—Sir Gilbert Crump was there too. I remember he said it was *magnificent* how Jasper Blow had really got a move on by cutting something called red-tape, whatever that means, and that Querbury was proud to be the scene of . . ." she faltered.

"I know," I said. "*Of what may become a turning point in the national campaign to solve the traffic problem.*"

"Yes, that's right. How did you know?"

But Sasha glared at me, and I said: "Never mind. Do go on, please."

"Well, then it was rather awful because Sir Gilbert Crump looked at Peter and said: 'How proud you must be, young fellow, of your father and your uncle.' Peter had been totally silent throughout. I supposed he was just shy. So I was just as shocked as everyone when he burst out angrily: 'Personally, I think it's a scandal putting the road south of the Beacon, when it should obviously go to the north—through *here*. And I don't think my father has the faintest idea of what's been going on over this road behind the scenes or how much resentment and injustice it will cause locally. He's too busy blowing his own trumpet.'"

"Golly, good for P. Blow," I exclaimed. "What happened?"

"Well, everyone looked aghast, but luckily my mother roared with laughter and said: "My dear Peter, you're adorably idealistic. Don't you realise that if the road came *this* side of the Beacon you wouldn't be eating that delicious pheasant? And then everyone laughed, at least laughed it off, and Sir Gilbert Crump said he remembered being a rebel himself at the same age and that it was a healthy sign, though he didn't explain what it was a healthy sign *of*."

In the five years I'd known her, I'd never heard Helen string so many words intelligibly together. I was impressed and offered her some more cocoa.

"Yes, please, if there's any left. Not too much brandy, though. I can drink any amount of whisky, but brandy goes to my head." She giggled.

"What happened after that?" Sasha asked.

"Well, I'm afraid Peter got a *terrific* blowing-up—ha, ha,

forgive the pun—from his uncle on the way home, but that only made him more rebellious. We still went on seeing a lot of each other, so I heard about it and what he wanted to do." She paused and hiccuped. "Oh, dear, I'm not sure I should really tell you the rest."

I said: "Do go on, I won't breathe a word." (Nor have I, I might add, till this minute.)

She went on: "Well, you see, apparently Peter had found out that his father and uncle had pushed the road business through *much* faster than they should have done really. I mean by law. His father is quite honest, of course, but tremendously ambitious. His uncle is also tremendously ambitious, but—well, perhaps not *quite* so honest. For instance, Peter discovered his uncle stood to make a lot of money out of the road—I don't really understand why. Peter felt the family honour was at stake somehow—I don't really understand that either—and that it was up to him. . . ."

I couldn't remain silent a minute longer. "You mean it was *Peter* who bashed the bulldozers!"

Helen tittered. "Yes. But only the first night. He'd warned me on Saturday he was going to, and I didn't believe him. Actually, he rode there on Sunday morning, but someone was in the quarry, so he had to go away and come back. He took a canvas bucket specially and poured the water with that. We didn't meet again over the week-end, in fact till this morning when we had lunch together in Querbury. That's when he told me. Of course, I accused him of having done it last night too, but he swears he didn't. He said he wanted to, in fact he meant to creep out on foot last night, but he overslept. So he was just as amazed by the news to-day as everyone else."

A fantastic suspicion crossed my mind, but I kept it to myself and begged Helen to tell us what had happened to-day after lunch.

"Well, the plan was for Captain Gumble to drive us home after the film, for tea at Deans. He told us to come at one-forty-five to an office in a funny old alley, so as to fix a rendezvous for later. We met him there. A couple called Bunn were also there—they're connected with him in some way I don't grasp. But Peter *did* grasp. As I've said, I don't understand why he feels his uncle has behaved dishonourably, but he *does* feel it—terribly—that's why he got fed up watching the film. He wanted to walk and talk. I didn't, because of the snow. We stood outside the cinema squabbling and Peter became quite horrid—I'd never seen him like that. Then Captain Gumble himself came past, going to his car. Peter left me and went up to him. They stood in the pelting snow and seemed to be having a flaming row. I heard Peter shout: ' Unless you call it off I'll go to the police.' Then Captain Gumble simply pushed Peter furiously aside, got in the car and drove away. And Peter ran madly into the police station next door. I didn't wait. I was so frightened I started to run myself— for home. I don't know Querbury very well and what with the snow and the dark I went in the wrong direction. Then some rude boys threw snowballs. . . ." Helen's head nodded. " Then I got lost and that delish . . . that delishush young man . . ."

Sasha and I looked at one another and giggled. " Golly, she's passed out," I said.

" Best let her sleep till my mother comes."

Mrs. Henry arrived soon afterwards and we told her quickly what had happened, without going into *all* the details.

" We can't leave her here. But this snow is really heavy,

it will be worse at Marsh Manor, and I'd rather get you back first, February. We'll wrap her up well and put her in the car. I'll take her home after I've dropped you."

We carried her out and dumped her like a sack of flour on the back seat. Helen didn't stir an eyelid. I guessed I'd rather overdone the brandy in the cocoa!

Chapter 17

MRS. HENRY drove carefully out of the town along the Chichester Road. In the headlights, the snow seemed to be hailing down on the windscreen like a million angry white insects. It had settled deeply in places on the road—there wasn't enough traffic to disperse it. Soon after we left Querbury a green car travelling fast overtook us. We saw the silhouette of two men in front.

"Looks like Jim," Mrs. Henry said. "I suppose he's been called out in a hurry, poor dear. I wonder who's with him."

We passed the Henrys' gates, then lights winked in the outlying houses of Brampton, as we cautiously approached the dangerous bend near Mrs. Bunn's stores. Suddenly Mrs. Henry jammed on her brakes. A policeman stood in the road waving a torch. She opened the window.

"Pull into the side, please," he ordered. "There's been a pile-up just ahead."

"I'm Mrs. Henry—Dr. Henry's wife. He was in front of us just now, I think." Her voice trembled.

"That's all right, Mrs. Henry. Your husband's just arrived. We sent for him. Where are you trying to reach?"

"Marsh Manor."

"Then you can carry on and up the side road—you'll get by all right."

Feeling as if I might be sick any second, I leaned across and shouted: "I'm Mr. Callendar's daughter. It's nothing to do with him, is it?"

"Nothing at all. Don't worry, miss," the policeman said in a calm reassuring voice and waved us on.

We crept past two or three cars drawn up, including Dr. Henry's. A police car was parked at the junction, its headlights turned full on to Mrs. Bunn's stores where a crowd of bystanders had gathered in spite of the blizzard. We didn't want to look and yet had to—as you do. But at first we couldn't see any sign of an accident.

Then we caught a glimpse of an extraordinary sight. The back end of a large black saloon stuck out of the shop window. The bonnet must have reached the counter.

Mrs. Henry halted her car ten yards up the side road. "Stay in the car with Helen, both of you. I just want to see if there's anything I can do."

"Shall I come too? I'm pretty good at first-aid," I offered —rather gallantly, I thought. But she snapped my head off. "Do as you're told. I'll be back directly." She slammed the door and vanished. "I only wanted to help," I muttered crossly to Sasha, who just sat white and silent beside me.

A man opened the door and poked his head inside. "Is that you, February? Thought I recognised the voice." It was Mr. Mitchell, our gardener.

"That's Captain Gumble's car, isn't it?"

"Afraid so. Proper shambles. He missed me by inches— I was just going in to buy some tobacco." Mr. Mitchell sounded pretty shaken.

"Is he badly hurt?"

" Gonner, I should think. And Mrs. Bunn too, I'm afraid. She was standing by the counter. Just got back from Querbury herself, someone said. Hadn't even taken her hat off. Her husband had dropped her and gone off round the farm. We're trying to find him now."

" But what happened? " Sasha asked.

" Going too fast at that bend mostly. He must know the bend well enough too. Funny thing—I heard the car coming and felt sort of queer—had the same feeling once in the war before a shell landed. I stepped back. Else I'd have copped it, I reckon."

" Did he skid? "

" No, went slap ahead. But it wasn't just the weather blinded him." Mr. Mitchell stood there half in the car, half out, scratching his chin and taking no notice of the snow piling on his back. " No one I've told this to believes me, but it's the truth. The swans killed the captain—that is, if he does die."

" The swans! "

" Six or seven of 'em. They've been up and down this valley all the year. Now they'd lost themselves in the snow, I reckon—perhaps even mistook the road for the river. They swooped down from nowhere suddenly, past the car's wind-screen—right at the bend when he should have been turning —it's a wonder they weren't hit—must have scared the captain out of his wits for a moment."

" More than for a moment," I thought, but didn't like to say so. Instead I asked if everything was all right at Marsh Manor.

" Busy day up there with visitors. Coming and going all morning. Reporters and such-like. Reckon Sprocketts will give up the road in this weather," he added. Another man had approached the car and Mr. Mitchell withdrew. It turned out to be my friend the Scotland Yard detective. He came and sat on the driving-seat, closing the door.

" We meet again. You'll have gathered what's happened? "

" Yes. Is he dead? "

" Not quite. In fact, Dr. Henry thinks he'll pull through. We're waiting for the ambulance."

" What about Mrs. Bunn? "

" *She'll* be all right—just bruises and concussion. She's talking—and how! "

" Interesting talk, I should imagine," I said.

" Very, as a matter of fact."

" Shall I give you a tip? I mean, Scotland Yard doesn't *mind* being helped? "

" Not in the least—if it doesn't take too long. Snow's got into my neck."

" Well, then, if Captain Gumble's unconscious, I suggest you take his fingerprints! "

The detective's face was clearly visible in the light from the police car's headlights and I saw him start. He looked at me hard.

" Funny you should say that. Our mutual friend Mike Spillergun suggested exactly the same thing just now."

" Is *he* here? "

" Oh, yes, Mike's here—came along in Dr. Henry's car. They happened to be together at the hospital when we rang there."

" And *did* you take them? The fingerprints, I mean."

The detective leant towards us farther and whispered: " It's against regulations. But, yes, February Callendar, as a matter of fact, I *did*. When no one was looking. And examined them in the shop. And they're *not* the same as any of those on the saucepan, if *that's* what you were thinking."

" No, I didn't think that. But weren't there fingerprints left last night too—by whoever put sand in the engines? "

" Unfortunately not—you don't get fingerprints on frozen objects, though frost can't remove ones already there. Those engines were freezing hard all through last night. No prints . . ."

I must have shown my disappointment, for he added: " I follow the train of thought, but you're wrong. So instead of that ice-cream I promised, I'll give you a hint. Remember the cockney foreman at the quarry? If I tell you his name is Thorpe, does that ring a bell?"

" Mrs. Bunn's brother!"

The detective chuckled. "No flies on you, February."

" Do you think she might have put him up to it? Has she said anything—while she's concussed?"

" She's said plenty. But not about that especially. She appears to be chiefly concerned whether the Government goes ahead with the trunk road."

Sasha nudged me and I nudged her back. "Do you think her brother—Thorpe—could have damaged the bulldozers the first night too?" I asked.

" Let's assume he did—makes it all much easier." I wondered if he really knew who had done it that time.

I asked if they'd caught Thorpe yet.

" Not yet. Doubt if we'll bother. Depends whether there's to be a prosecution about the bulldozers. Something tells me there won't."

Sasha leant over and said: "I say, when you went rushing after Captain Gumble, was it because you thought he might be doing a bunk—out of the country?"

" Now we really are getting into deep waters. If you must know, he'd borrowed my fountain-pen and I wanted it back."

" Oh, ha, ha!" I said. "Peter Blow ran into the police station to warn you his uncle was driving off. I suppose you happened to be there at the time. You have a habit of being in the police station at the right moment!"

That really shook him. "Mike Spillergun's right, by golly. The sooner we get you working for us at Scotland Yard, the sooner we'll get the crime wave under control. Thank goodness, here's Mrs. Henry." He climbed out of the car to let her in.

"It's not as bad as it looked," she said briskly. "I'll drive you home first and then I'll deal with Helen. Has she stirred?"

"No, drunk as a lord, lucky girl," Sasha said.

Chapter 18

THE SNOW was worse along the lane near Marsh Manor. In the back of the car Helen woke up and didn't seem too well. She shivered and complained of a headache.

The family had finished tea when we arrived. We found my mother and Friday clearing up in the kitchen, while Hildebrand crawled around polishing the lino. Gail was still upstairs in bed and Berry, Chrys and Des had rushed off to play records in the barn. After a hurried consultation between the two mothers it was decided to keep Helen warm in our house and telephone Lady Sprockett. With Friday's help we lugged her indoors and tucked her up with more rugs on the living-room sofa, where she immediately fell asleep again.

Lady Sprockett took it calmly, and said she would drive round and collect Helen as soon as she had finished some rather delicious *pâté* sandwiches.

We made fresh tea and toast, and settled down to exchange news round the kitchen table.

"Jim said he'd come straight on here once the ambulance had been to fetch Captain Gumble. He can look at Helen then," said Mrs. Henry.

Of course my mother and Friday hadn't heard of the accident. In fact, they and Mrs. Henry were completely out of touch with the whole situation as Sasha and I knew it.

" Will Captain Gumble pull through?" my mother asked.

" Jim thought he probably would—but it will be a long job, I'm afraid."

" Perhaps this will *force* the Council to do something at last about that bend, even if the trunk road is held up for the present. I can't believe they'll carry on in this snow."

" Sasha and I think Captain Gumble was doing a bunk out of England and the police were after him. That's why he was going so fast," I said.

" Why ever should he do a bunk?" Mrs. Henry asked, and my mother exclaimed:

" My dear child, what rubbish you talk."

" It jolly well is *not* rubbish," I began—but there was too much to explain that she didn't yet know about! Instead I told them how we'd seen Mr. Mitchell in Brampton and how the car had nearly run into him. I repeated his story of the swans. " He said no one believed him, but he swore it was true."

" I don't see why not. He's the last man to imagine things," said my mother. And Friday added: " Accidents are frequently caused by birds—I read an article about it in *Elizabethan*."

" Mr. Mitchell also told us you'd had a lot of visitors here all day," said Sasha.

" The place has been a madhouse. Reporters from pretty well all the papers. Gus and John Gubbins turned up too, for a moment. I'm expecting them back any minute. They had a conference this afternoon in Querbury with Gilbert Crump and Jasper Blow."

" My dear, you should have let me have the children for you," said Mrs. Henry. " You must be dead."

" Luckily they've been no trouble. Friday's been up at the

quarry with Robin Fawcett and his friends. The others have spent the whole day playing records in the barn. Ah, here they are. Mind the *snow*!" she shouted, as the three younger girls came rushing in through the outside kitchen door, letting the blizzard in after them and then shaking the snow off over the floor.

" You like playing records, I hear," said Mrs. Henry. " It's super fun," they agreed.

" I should think the records will be worn out before we need them to-morrow—though I can't imagine *anyone* will come to the dance in this," said my mother.

Mrs. Henry slapped a hand to her forehead. " My dear, don't say the dance is *to-morrow*? I thought it was to-morrow *week*! In fact, I looked at the card only this morning."

" I thought it was next Wednesday too," Sasha said.

" And it's funny because earlier this afternoon I happened to overhear Helen talking to P. Blow about the dance and *they* both thought it was next week," I added.

Now it was my mother's turn to slap her forehead. She stared at us all aghast. " But . . . I wrote all the cards out by hand—one evening before the holidays started. I did a few spares too, for last minute invitations like P. Blow and Helen. I believe there are still one or two on my desk."

Poor Mummy. She rushed out of the kitchen to the living-room and came back like someone who had seen a ghost, with a card in her hand. She was half laughing, half in tears.

" Wednesday 19*th* January. Oh, *no*! How *could* I have got it wrong! "

Both Friday and I put an arm round her and said: " *Please* don't mind. This is the most marvellous piece of news this hols!" And Mrs. Henry said: "My dear, try and see the funny side. Probably the snow will have gone in a week, so it will be all for the best."

"*Exactly,*" Friday and I shouted together. "We both go back to school on the 18*th*, so what could be better! You must write and tell us all about it."

But my mother just said broken-heartedly: "*Children.* I sometimes wonder whether they're worth it."

"Of course we're worth it," Berry said. "We're a great consolation." And Chrys and Des, looking like angels, added: "*And* a blessing." And Hildebrand, not to be left out of things, knocked a full milk jug off the table over the floor.

We were still mopping, when a car's headlights flashed across the kitchen window. A moment later my father, John Gubbins and Mike Spillergun came into the kitchen, stamping the snow off, so that we had to do a lot more mopping.

"*How* many times must I ask you to use the front door, the garden door, the side door, *any* other door?" my mother protested.

"Oh, bother all doors!" my father laughed. "We've good news. Hallo, Olive and Sasha."

"Glad tidings of great joy I bring," said Mike Spillergun, giving an impersonation of an angel bringing glad tidings.

"In other words," said John Gubbins solemnly, "after a certain amount of pressure from us and Sir Gilbert Crump, the Minister of Highways has agreed to do a quick re-think on the whole subject of the trunk road. We left him doing it. Then on our way past Brampton we stopped at the accident and found this clown and brought him along."

"I must say dear old Gilbert Crump was splendid," said my

father. "After all, he's made some pretty pompous announcements supporting the road. Now he's changed round and supported us."

"Notwithstanding Crump," murmured Mike Spillergun, doing tricks to amuse the younger ones.

"Do you mean the road is cancelled?" I cried.

"Not quite that—at least not yet," said John Gubbins. "But there's bound to be the devil of a fuss in all the papers tomorrow, as Jasper Blow is well aware. Gilbert Crump urged him that the only honourable and sensible thing to do was to suspend work *immediately*, till he's given a public answer to the awkward questions."

"I like that!" I said. "The work has been suspended already in any case by the weather—not to mention by a few other things!"

And Friday said: "Oh, what a swizz. Robin promised to let me help up there. And I'd *so* looked forward to running the Callendar Chips and Comfort Station!"

"Of course, Jasper Blow never *will* answer the questions, whatever may be decided about the road," said my mother. "It will all be hushed up—and I for one will be thankful if it is. The sooner we can forget it and settle down again to normal life the better."

"I dare say you're right," said John Gubbins. "To be fair to Jasper Blow, he's an excellent Minister. He's just a little over-anxious to get things *done*—which, after all, is a fault on the right side. And perhaps he's also been a little unwise in his choice of brothers-in-law. . . . We can't stop the rest of the Press having their fun to-morrow, but the *Messenger* is dropping its attack—for the present. We've some rather unpleasant facts and in return for not publishing them we've asked the

Minister to reconsider whether perhaps the road shouldn't go *north* of Querbury Beacon after all. . . ."

" What's happening about Sprocketts' bulldozers then?" I asked.

" Nothing at all, I suspect. Lord Sprockett has told the police he doesn't intend to prosecute. Too many things might come to light that he'd rather were kept in the dark, I dare say——"

" So no one knows who actually *did* bash the bulldozers *either* night?" Friday said. Sasha and I exchanged a wink.

" The police are certain it was that cockney foreman both nights. Thorpe's his name, I think. Apparently he had a grudge against Captain Gumble and the Downland Preservation Company. We chatted to a Scotland Yard detective in Brampton just now, when we picked Mike up, and according to him there's not really enough evidence against Thorpe for the police to prosecute him on their own. The Irishman is pretty vague what happened. He just assumes Thorpe hit him, but he can't prove it. You spoke to him, Mike, didn't you? "

" Oh, yes, Dr. Henry and I and a police sergeant all questioned Paddy in the hospital, but we got nowhere. I gather he and Thorpe just sat drinking, through the night, taking it in turns to stroll round with the dog. The police theory is that Thorpe got cold and fed up and simply pushed off half-way through, having done the damage. But that doesn't explain why he should have crowned Paddy."

" I see." Not that I did, all the same.

" How's Gail?" Daddy was saying to Mummy.

" Yes, how is dear Gail?" said Mrs. Henry. " I meant to ask."

" Goodness—I'd forgotten! " my mother exclaimed, in a voice which made everyone stop talking to listen. She spoke to Mrs. Henry, the way women always do speak to one another when it's a question of their children.

" As I told you on the phone, I noticed she looked rather white when the police came this morning. I thought it was nerves or a bilious attack and sent her to bed. She slept till lunch and her temperature was normal, but I could see she had something on her mind. I got it out of her at last. My dear, you'll never guess—the crazy child went off alone to the quarry in the middle of last night! "

" Good heavens! *Why?* " cried everyone, astounded.

" To keep up with her older sister, chiefly. She seems to have believed that February really *did* do the damage on Sunday night, so she decided to have a go on her own! " Mummy turned to me.

" I gather you called her wet the other day. Gail's *very* sensitive—you simply must be more careful, darling, what you say to her."

" Well, *really*! I like that! "

" Jolly plucky of her, all the same," said Friday. " I mean, she knew there would be a guard on, as well as the dog. Captain Gumble warned us himself."

" Yes. She thought she could manage the dog and hoped the men would be dozing."

" But how on earth did she propose to do the damage? " asked my father. " Not with water again? "

" Oh, she hadn't any plan. She just went to see what she could do." My mother shuddered. " Of all the mad ideas— I can hardly bear to think what might have happened."

" But what *did* happen? Surely it wasn't her who put the

sand in the engines?" I said. I confess I was feeling quite sick with envy at Gail having scored off me.

"No, of course not. Nothing at all happened, as far as I can make out. There were three men talking, she says. After creeping around she obviously lost her nerve and came away —thank goodness she did."

"*Three* men . . ." said my father. "Who was the third?"

"Yes. Who?" cried several of us at once.

"I haven't the least idea. Nor has she, I imagine."

"I know *exactly* who it was, thanks very much!"

Gail stood behind us in the door, having heard the last sentence or two. She wore a dressing-gown over her pyjamas and didn't look in the least white or ill now—just rather pleased with herself.

My mother began to fuss about her not being in bed, but I shouted impatiently: "*Who?*" as if I hadn't guessed. In fact, I think we all knew the answer.

"Captain Gumble."

"Dear me," said John Gubbins.

"How extremely interesting," said my father. But Mike Spillergun just looked dreamily at the ceiling, puffing smoke-rings to amuse the little ones.

"The three men were talking beside one of the bulldozers. I crept right up close," Gail told us, enjoying every minute of her star role—as she well deserved to. "Ginger actually came and sniffed at me, and I patted him on the head and he went off again."

"Did you hear what they were saying?" asked Mrs. Henry.

"Oh, yes. Captain Gumble told them he was awfully sorry to keep them out on such a cold night and that he'd come to do his share, and they could now go. One of the others—the smaller one—said he'd had quite enough and drove away on a motor bike. But the larger man, who sounded a bit *funny*, told Captain Gumble to go to hell and said he intended to stay, now he was there."

"And then——?" we all asked breathlessly.

"Well . . . nothing, really. They walked off arguing and I didn't see how I could damage the bulldozers with Captain Gumble around. Anyway, I was jolly cold and frightened by then, so I came back."

"Darling, you're never, *never* to do such a silly thing again, do you understand?" Mummy said, putting an arm round her. "Now go straight upstairs and get back into bed!"

"Oh, but I'm feeling fine now!" Gail insisted. After an argument she was allowed to stay.

"Now perhaps you'll admit that it wasn't rubbish—what Sasha and I thought about Captain Gumble doing a bunk!" I said triumphantly.

My father and John Gubbins had to have all that part of it explained—though Sasha and I didn't breathe a word of what Helen had told us in the surgery.

"Whatever Captain Gumble may have done I feel he's been sufficiently punished," said my mother. "So I suggest we keep what Gail has told us to ourselves."

We all agreed with that.

"So there won't be a special Mike Spillergun column to-morrow?" Sasha said.

"No. My lips are sealed," Mike answered in a melancholy voice. "But at least I can be sure of getting to February's dance."

"*There isn't going to be a dance!*" we all shouted, laughing.

That had to be explained.

" I've sweated blood decorating the blasted barn all for nothing! " Daddy groaned. I could see he was secretly as relieved as we were.

" Do you mean I shan't be able to do my sword-swallowing act after all, *or* dance Sir Roger de Eiderdown? " Mike said, looking as if it was the greatest disappointment of his life.

" Let's have a party to-night instead—just for all of us," I suggested.

" Did someone say *party*? May *I* come? "

Lady Sprockett had appeared unannounced behind us. She had driven to the front of the house and let herself in.

" Of course," Mummy said. " Except that probably you'll want to take Helen back home."

" Nothing I want to do less—if there's going to be a *party*. Anyway, *she's* all right—that divine doctor is tickling her ribs with a stethoscope now. We arrived together."

" How odd to hear my husband called divine," said Mrs. Henry, not very cordially—she had never met Lady Sprockett and didn't know the form.

But Lady Sprockett answered charmingly: " My dear, I envy you. I wish he was mine. Look, I happen to have a couple of bottles of champagne in the boot of the car. Never travel without. So let me just ask your husband if I can leave Helen on that sofa for another hour and I'll fetch them." We heard her switch the full horse-power of her charm on to Dr. Henry in the living-room.

Mike Spillergun caught my eye, and we both burst out laughing suddenly.

" What's the big joke? " Daddy asked him.

" I was just wondering how a certain Mr. Bunthorpe is

going to feel when he hears the road may not be built this side of the downs after all. . . . I fancy February and Sasha are wondering much the same."

" Bunthorpe? That chap who's managing director of the D.P.C.? Do you know him?"

" Oh, yes. . . . Not well. But we know him," said Mike.

" Oh, yes, we know him," said Sasha and I.

Daddy looked slightly mystified. " I've never met him myself. Lucky for him he sold out to Gumble, if the road *doesn't* go this side. Poor Gumble, he'll lose a packet on all this. At least he'll be glad I returned the cheque the D.P.C. offered for half the paddock."

So we told him who Bunthorpe really was and how it was he, or rather they, who looked like losing the packet!

" But now you won't get compensation *either* for the paddock *or* for the canal tunnel road!" Friday interrupted. That boy thinks of nothing but money.

" True, I shan't. But I'm in funds again. The *Messenger* has paid a large cheque for what it owes me, and a publisher has commissioned me to write a book. I've even managed to settle your next term's school fees!"

" What's the book about?" I asked.

Daddy grinned sheepishly. " About the need to treat the whole traffic problem as a national emergency, and to build really good modern roads." He had the grace to blush.

" I'm afraid I've begun to wonder if it's *possible* to have good roads in this country," said John Gubbins, smiling. " Hitler and Mussolini built them—it's the only good thing they did. But the price was too high. Roads seem to be incompatible with the democratic way of life."

" I'm sick of roads," said my mother. " But there are still

two points I'd like to know. Do you think the cockney *did* pour water down the exhaust pipes on Sunday night? It's incredible to think his rage was put on when he came here."

" Must have been," said my father; and John Gubbins said, " Let's assume he did—it makes things easier."

Sasha and I said nothing.

" What's the second point? " asked Mrs. Henry.

" Well, I can see that after Mike Spillergun's article this morning Captain Gumble must have realised the game was up and the road probably wouldn't be built. But he didn't know that *last night*. So what was his object in putting the bull-dozers out of action for a further day or two?"

None of us apparently could think of an answer to that. Mike Spillergun went on playing unconcernedly with the younger ones, tossing up sugar lumps and catching them in his mouth.

" It certainly is a good point," said John Gubbins. " Mike, you know more than anyone about Gumble's activities. What do *you* think? "

" Oh, I don't think. I'm just a humble columnist." And he threw three lumps up together, catching them all. " Still . . ." He spoke somewhat inaudibly while he munched. " Like every other contractor, Sprocketts were insured against damage and delay. Very heavily insured, considering the sums involved, I should imagine. Sprockett's area manager, and we know who that is, put in an immediate claim for the hold-up yesterday. I expect he put another claim in this morning as well—if he had the time."

" How did you find that one out? "

" The Insurance Company consulted a friend of mine in Scotland Yard."

" So *that's* what the detective was really doing down here! "
I said.

" I expect you find the grown-up world a bit puzzling, don't
you, February? " said Mike. " Mortgages, insurance swindles,
trunk roads . . ."

But Lady Sprockett re-entered with the two bottles, one
under each arm. Dr. Henry was behind her.

" The Doctor says I can safely leave Helen on the sofa for
another hour. Incidentally, she reeks of brandy. Did I hear
someone talking about the road? "

" Yes," my mother said. " It seems likely now that it won't
come past here after all."

" Where will it go then? " Lady Sprockett handed the
bottles to Dr. Henry for him to open.

" Well, there's a theory that it should go *north* of Querbury
Beacon . . ." Mike Spillergun said innocently.

" Really? That's what Captain Gumble's nice nephew said
too—Peter Blow. Heavens! I've forgotten him. He's been
in the car all this time listening to the radio. I found him
walking to Dippenhall—said he'd lost Helen and was trying to
catch up with her. Such devotion. He must be frozen. Friday,
be an angel and go and bring him in quickly."

Friday went off sheepishly to fetch the Head of his House.
The champagne was opened and glasses handed round. Lady
Sprockett sipped hers, then addressed us all.

" I say, if anyone tries to put that trunk road through Deans,
I'll fight them tooth and nail. ' You've gotta fight sometime '
—as a young friend of mine was quoted as saying in the cheap
press this morning."

" The road's got to go *somewhere*," John Gubbins said.

" Nonsense. Much better let people kill themselves—it keeps

down the surplus population. This island's overcrowded. Besides, we won't need roads in a few more years—they'll be as old-fashioned as motor cars."

The front door opened and shut. Friday and P. Blow could be heard running together through the hall towards the kitchen.

" You'll never guess! " Friday gasped, coming in.

" It was on the news! " P. Blow cried.

" The Russians! " Friday said.

" No, the Americans! " P. Blow contradicted him.

" I'm *sure* he said the Russians, Peter."

" No, I'm certain it was the Americans, Friday."

" *What?* " we *all* yelled at them.

" They've landed a man on the Moon! " Friday and P. Blow said together.

" *Bon spectacle*, as the French say," I said.

" Thank God it's only that," my mother said. " For a moment I was afraid something important had happened."

Hildebrand upset another jug of milk.